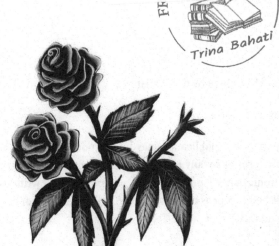

SAVING
SCARLETT

C.A. VARIAN

Book Cover by Artscandare Cover Design

Hard Cover by Leigh Graphic Design

Special Edition Dust Jacket Art by hmmr.art on Instagram

Editing by Willow Oak Author Services and Kristen Winiarski

Internal Formatting by C.A. Varian

Page Edge Design by Painted Wings Publishing Services

1st edition 2024

To Irina,

♡

aVarian

for anyone who's ever had a
significant other who just
needed to be T*KEN THE
f#CK OUT...
And for those who finally got
their freedom...

this book is for you.

CAVarian

Trigger Warnings

There are many mature themes throughout Saving Scarlett. It is not intended for readers under 17 years of age.

The following themes are explored in this book and are not limited to: graphic (consensual) sexual content, graphic domestic violence, abduction, graphic descriptions of aberrant violence and torture, vulgar language, and murder.

Cajun
Pronunciations

Cher: shă (Pet name like darling)

Beignet: bin yay

Fouchon: foo shaan

mon joli petit amant:
ma 'ZHōlē pə'tēt amã

Mon amant assassin:
ma amã ə'sas(ə)n

CHAPTER 1

The Survivor

"**S**car, wake up."

Hearing my friend Ashley's voice, my eyes fluttered open, my neck cramping as I tried to lift my head. The chair beneath me was not fit for sleeping. "What time is it?"

Not answering right away, she moved across my office and opened the shades, the sun nearly blinding me. "It's eight in the morning. Damn, Scar. Did you stay here all night?"

"Huh? Eight..." My words trailed off as I got ahold of my senses. There was a reason I'd slept at my bookstore, Tangled in the Pages, but not one I was willing to share, not even with her. "I worked late trying to get inventory done and food prep for the store before morning shift, but I hadn't intended to sleep here."

Shaking her head, Ashley placed a cup of coffee in my hand. "Do you want to go home and change? Maybe put some ice on that. How in the hell did you do that to yourself?"

When she pointed at my face, I lost all ability to breathe, my lungs seizing as images of what had happened the day before flooded into my head—the beating he'd given me—again. I lifted my fingers to my cheek, touching the area where my eye was swollen. Grinning, I feigned embarrassment. No one knew my shameful secret. "Oh. Yeah. I took a book to the eye last night. I must not have pushed it all the way onto the shelf."

Ashley turned a side eye in my direction. "You know I'll help you with inventory. All you have to do is ask. Especially since you seem to keep getting more and more clumsy these days. How old are you again? Eighty?"

Huffing a laugh, I took a deep sip of the coffee, closing my eyes as it fed my caffeine addiction. "I'm thirty and I was just tired. That's what I get for working so late every night, but I can't seem to help myself. This place is my dream, after all."

While I dug in my purse for headache medication, she left my office and began working on the opening procedures.

Once Ashley put the money into the register, she returned to me, looking more closely at my injury. I hissed as she touched it, even though her hand was gentle.

"You may need to have that looked at in case you have a concussion. And go home at night, Scar. Work can wait until the next morning."

I grinned and nodded. There was so much I wanted to tell my friend but couldn't, or at least, *wouldn't*. "I'll go home and take a shower. Are you sure you'll be okay while I'm gone? Can I bring you back something to eat?"

With a shake of her head, she all but shoved me toward the door. "We have pastries here. I'll be fine. Now go and get yourself presentable and put on lots of concealer."

When I got in my car, I checked my phone and was relieved to have no messages. My husband, Joshua, knew I was at the store and had not called to check up on me. I wasn't surprised. He'd probably gone straight to his mistress the moment I'd left the house. All I hoped was that he wasn't home when I got there.

Sucking in a breath as my reality threatened to pour fresh tears out of my bruised eye, I turned up the radio, hoping the music could drown out the thoughts running through my head, all of them telling me to run away.

Since no one was home when I arrived at my house, I took a quick shower and packed an overnight bag, just in case I fell asleep in my bookstore again. It didn't have a bed, but it was still a safe place where I could hide out when I needed to.

By the time I made it back to Tangled in the Pages, my bookstore and coffee shop combo was in full swing. Ashley was taking orders while another employee, Jack, was preparing the food and drinks. Ashley looked up at me as the bell jingled over the door, her eyes telling me they were swamped and needed help. It was the exact reason I had been hesitant to leave in the first place.

Tossing my bags in my office and locking the door, I returned to the front of the store and took over register duty so Ashley could help Jack. With the holidays coming, it was our busiest time of year, which made me wonder if I needed to hire a few more employees to help during the rushes. I'd only had the store for a few years, so it was still a new adventure for me.

I moved to the counter, pouring fresh coffee and greeting customers with practiced ease. The familiar routine calmed my frayed nerves, allowing me to push aside the lingering fear and anxiety. I was safe there in my space, surrounded by the things and people I loved.

"The usual?" I asked an older gentleman, Henry, who came in every morning. He nodded, eyes crinkling behind wire-rimmed glasses.

"You're a lifesaver, cher." His voice was warm, full of affection. "Don't know what I'd do without my morning coffee and chat."

"You'd find another coffee shop," I teased, sliding his coffee across the counter and waving away his attempt to pay. "On the house today, Henry. You deserve it."

"Well, aren't you a sweetheart." Smile deepening, he patted my hand before moving to the chair by the window and burying himself in the newspaper I always set aside for him.

Bumping my shoulder, Ashley nodded at the few customers waiting to be served. "You okay?"

"Yeah." I drew in a steadying breath, meeting her concerned gaze. "I'm okay. Just tired."

"I'm here if you need anything." Her brown eyes were warm, full of affection. She'd been with me since the beginning. "Always."

"I know." I smiled, small but genuinely. "Thank you. For everything."

Smiling, she nudged me again. "Anytime. Now come on, time to get back to work!"

I laughed, following her lead as we set about serving the new customers who'd lined up at the register. With the warmth of an environment I created myself, the familiar routine eased the lingering ache in my chest.

Once the morning rush had calmed, I wiped the dust from the shelves and straightened the stacks of books, admiring my cozy bookstore. The aroma of fresh coffee wafted through the air, mingling with the soft jazz music playing over the speakers. Even if I hadn't owned the store, I realized I would probably spend all my time there. It was the exact way I wanted my customers to feel.

My muscles ached from unloading inventory for hours the night before, but a familiar peace settled over me. My bookstore was my sanctuary, a refuge from a world that had been cruel and unforgiving for too long.

As I bustled around the space, a young couple lounged on the sofa near the fireplace, sipping lattes and reading from well-worn paperbacks. The fireplace didn't get much use, since it was hot as Hades in Louisiana most of the year, but it was still a beautiful feature of the building. Two teenage girls giggled over their cinnamon rolls at a table near the front window and an older man tapped away on his laptop in the corner, a half-empty mug of Earl Grey tea beside him. *My regulars.* They came for the atmosphere as much as for the books and coffee.

Leaning against the counter, I breathed in the familiar scents, feeling tension ease from my shoulders. My gaze wandered to the worn wooden floors and shelves lining the walls, filled with stories of adventure, heartbreak and hope. There were so many lives and worlds contained within the pages to get lost in. I only wished I had more time to read.

A smile tugged at my lips as another wave of customers trickled through the door. My perfect, imperfect world. The one I had built from nothing.

This was my story.

My happily ever after.

Joshua couldn't take that away from me.

Noticing that a group of college kids had left a stack of books on a small table near the back of the store, which was a daily occurrence, I scooped them up, intending to put them away. I had just started returning them to the shelves when the bell above the door chimed, drawing my gaze. A man stepped inside, tall and broad-shouldered, clad in black from head to toe. Jet black hair fell over piercing blue eyes as he paused just inside the entrance, scanning the room. His gaze was sharp, intense, taking in everything and missing nothing.

Unease flickered through me at his imposing presence, at odds with the cozy atmosphere of my shop. And yet...curiosity stirred as I studied him from beneath my lashes. There was a hardness to his expression, as if he had seen and endured far too much in his life, although he couldn't have been much older than me. But something about his lingering gaze and the way one corner of his mouth tilted upward tugged at my interest and I had to admit, he was sexy as hell.

A mystery waiting to be solved.

His gaze landed on a shelf of tattered paperbacks along the far wall and the hint of a smile softened his angular features. My heart skipped as he strode forward, boots thudding against the wooden floor, and slid out a worn copy of *Treasure Island*.

Interest sparked in those fathomless light blue eyes as he flipped through the pages, as if transported to another time and place. A place of adventure and danger and...*longing*.

Heat crept into my cheeks. I was reading too much into a simple glance and smile, letting my imagination run wild. The stranger was just a customer, here to browse the shelves like any other.

Surprising even myself, I moved across the room, my hands smoothing the front of my apron as I stepped forward to greet him.

I cleared my throat, my pulse quickening like I was an unpopular schoolgirl asking the popular guy to prom. "Find anything interesting?"

Glancing up from the book, a flicker of surprise crossed his expression, as if he hadn't expected me to approach. Still, his lips curved into a slow, devastating smile that did dangerous things to my heart.

"A childhood favorite." As though fate only meant to be crueler, his voice was as smooth and dark as aged whiskey. He held up the book. "Treasure Island ignited my love for adventure at a young age."

"Mine as well." I leaned a hip against the shelf, hoping I appeared more at ease than I felt. Inside, my body was buzzing. "The pirates, the danger, the thrill of discovering treasure. Stevenson was a master storyteller."

"That he was." Sliding the book back into place, he turned to face me fully, arms loosely crossing over his chest. Even with my heels, I had to tilt my head back to meet his gaze.

"You have an interesting collection here. Not what one would expect in a small coffee shop."

"I'm glad you think so." Although I shrugged, a flush of pride rushed through me. "Books have always been my passion. There's nothing quite like getting lost in a good story, discovering new worlds and characters."

"An escape from reality." His tone had gone pensive, as if he understood that need on a deeper level. "And a glimpse into the lives of others, to remind us we're not alone."

I stared at him, struck by the insight. He saw it, the power of stories—of words—to transcend our circumstances and forge connections.

A slow smile curved my lips. "It seems we have more in common than a love for *Treasure Island*, Mr...?"

He blinked, as if realizing he hadn't introduced himself. "Bane."

Our gazes held for a long moment, a strange tension simmering between us. I couldn't look away from his eyes, pale blue and piercing, and I realized at that moment that his name was an omen. Something told me this man could destroy me and I would love every second of it.

Reminding myself that I was indeed married and that I shouldn't think such things, I licked my dry lips, all too aware of my heartbeat quickening. "Bane," I repeated. Even as I was berating myself for the awkward response, one corner of his mouth lifted in a half-smile that nearly threw my equilibrium off balance. "It's a pleasure."

"The pleasure is mine...?" He posed it as a question, obviously waiting for my name.

"I'm Scarlett."

Bane's gaze dipped to my mouth and then lower, a slow perusal that had heat pooling low in my belly. I shifted on my feet, torn between embarrassment at my reaction and a reckless urge to move closer to him, to close the space between us.

When his eyes returned to mine, a knowing glint lit their depths. As if he sensed the effect he had on me. As if he relished it. I didn't doubt he had that effect on all the ladies.

A blush stained my cheeks and I took a step back, breaking the spell. "Well," I said, a bit breathless, "let me know if you need any more book recommendations. I'm always here."

"I'll be sure to do that." Amusement lurked in his tone and he gave a slight bow of his head. "It was a pleasure meeting you, Scarlett."

Saving me from embarrassing myself any further, the bell above the door jingled, telling me new customers had entered the store. I smiled at him once more before turning to look back toward the counter, my hands twisting in my apron.

"That's my cue, but if you come to the register, I would be happy to give you a cup of coffee—on the house, of course. Since you have such good taste in books."

CHAPTER 2

The Savior

T he moonlight glinted off the blade of my favorite knife as I crept through the shadows toward my target. My footsteps were silent, my breathing steady. I was in my element.

Pausing behind a pillar, my eyes scanned the lavish ball-room before they fell on Auguste LaRoche, the corrupt businessman who had made far too many enemies. His receding hairline did nothing to hide the look of smug entitlement on his face as he laughed loudly with a group of partygoers. Little did he know those would be the last laughs he ever shared. Moving away from the group, he lifted his whiskey to his mouth, watching his guests.

I adjusted my grip on the knife, the leather of my gloves creaking ever so slightly. LaRoche's personal bodyguards stood several feet away, oblivious to the predator in their midst. *Fools.* Their complacency would cost their boss his life.

In one swift movement, I slipped behind LaRoche and pressed the cold steel to his throat, pulling him behind the pillar with me. His laughter transformed into a strangled gasp. The bodyguards whirled around, hands flying to their hip holsters, but they were too late. I'd already pulled him into a back hallway—out of sight.

"Please, I'll give you anything. Just don't—"

His begging turned into a gurgle as I slashed the knife across his throat, scarlet spilling down his white tuxedo shirt as he collapsed onto the white marble floor. As chaos erupted in the ballroom a moment later when his guards undoubtedly found him, I was already gone, disappearing into the night.

Another contract was completed. It was another day my niece would live to see, thanks to the funds from the night's kill. For her, I would paint the world red. For her, I would be a monster.

The sterile scent of antiseptic hit my nose as I walked through the automatic doors of the hospital. So late at night, the lights in the hallways were dimmed, the bustling crowds of the daytime replaced by the soft footsteps of nurses on night shift. I made my way to the pediatric intensive care unit, the one place in this world that made my chest constrict with emotion. It was past visiting hours, but no one ever stopped me from entering when I showed up. My money paid for part of their salary.

I nodded to the nurse at the desk before continuing to room four hundred and twenty-eight—Evelyn's room. Pushing the door open with a gentle hand, my eyes landed on my seven-year-old niece's tiny body lying motionless in the bed, the steady beep of the heart monitor the only indication she still clung to life. Her skin was pale, her bald head covered by a pink knitted cap. Dark circles stood out under her closed eyes, eyes that should have been filled with joy and laughter rather than pain.

Pulling a chair up next to her bed, I took her tiny hand in mine. So delicate, so fragile. Hard to believe that little hand once felt strong enough to grab onto my fingers as I swung her around the yard.

"Hey kiddo," I whispered. "I'm back."

No response, not that I expected one. The experimental treatment kept her unconscious most days, her body too weak to face the world. But I knew on some level she could sense I was there.

"I did it. I got the money for your next treatment." My voice caught, wishing I could take away her pain. "So, you just hang in there. You're going to get better soon, I promise."

Bringing her hand up to my lips, I kissed it before setting it back down. I had to believe she would recover. The alternative was too agonizing to face.

"I love you, Evie. Be strong for me."

I sat with her a while longer, keeping a silent vigil over her fragile form. For her, I would walk through the fires of hell. For her, I would make sure she survived—no matter the cost.

The door opened and I turned to see my sister entering, her black hair pulled back into a messy bun. Dark circles stood out under her eyes as well, testament to the many sleepless nights she'd spent at Evelyn's bedside.

Sitting beside me, Caroline placed a delicate hand on my shoulder. "She's fighting hard. Our girl's a warrior."

I nodded, a lump forming in my throat. Evelyn was the strongest person I knew, enduring endless treatments and pain with seldom a complaint.

Tapping the white, two-by-three piece of cardstock in my hand, I listened as the stiff-shirt CEO across from me droned on about the hit he wanted to take out on his unsuspecting wife and exactly how he wanted it done. Killing was my thing. It was the one thing I was really fucking good at, and I didn't need this asshole telling me how to do my job. Still, I didn't interrupt him. The more he spoke, the redder his face became, and I secretly hoped he would have a heart attack and keel over in his chair. I already had his payment in my pocket, a stack of unmarked bills that he wasn't getting back, even if he did croak in front of me.

Whenever I met with a potential client for the first time, I always tried to come up with their story in my head—first just to see how close I was—just to see how good I was at reading people. This guy was easy, no matter how hard he tried to convince me otherwise. He wanted to convince me that his wife was evil incarnate, the devil in disguise, but it all came down to greed. That's all it ever was for these white-collar assholes looking for a hit on their spouses.

From what I gathered, he wanted her out of the way, but he wanted to keep all the money. Simply put, his mistress was pregnant, and he wanted to marry her. Out with the old and in with the new. He knew if his wife found out, she would take him for all he was worth, but if she died... If his wife died in any way other than suicide, he would make a killing on her life insurance. *Pun intended.* Then, he would be able to marry his current mistress and find a new side piece as well. In other words, he would be able to move on with his life by repeating the cycle.

I could make it look like an accident or even a home robbery, and I wasn't there to question *why* he wanted her dead. There was no reason for him to tell me half of the shit that came tumbling out of his mouth. In my line of work, I tried to stay away from all that. I didn't care why someone ordered a hit or whether the target was a modern-day saint. My job was simple: take out the target and make money. Period. Whether his wife was the devil or the sweetest woman on the planet, I didn't give a shit. What he really needed was a therapist to talk to, even his barber would do, someone he could ramble to for a few hours to make him feel important. I had better things to do.

The underground club we sat in was a shady place in downtown New Orleans, but I'd chosen it specifically because I knew no one inside would speak a word of our meeting. Even though I didn't own the club, and the owner didn't even know my real name, he was indebted to me for a big job I'd done for him in the past. As far as the other patrons, most of them were so strung out that they wouldn't even remember being there themselves by the time they woke up in the morning, if they woke up at all.

As the clock ticked, I looked at my phone, pretending to get a message so he would get the hint that he needed to stop talking. "All I need to know is a general timeline and where to find her. I have to go, so if that's all..."

I pushed back in my chair, standing to leave, when he slid a slip of paper across the table. "This is my address. I'll be out of town next week at a business conference. She should be home alone then."

Thinking he was done speaking, *finally*, I turned to walk away when he grabbed my wrist.

I came very close to knocking him unconscious for touching me, but I clenched my jaw and turned back to look at him. "Don't ever put your hands on me," I growled, pulling out of his grip. "Not if you want to keep them."

Knowing what was good for him, he backed away, holding his hands up in supplication. "I'm sorry. I'm sorry. I just wanted to add the code to our security system so you can get inside the house."

Annoyance still boiling in my blood, I handed the paper back to him, scanning the club again as he scribbled some

24

digits onto it. We'd been in there for way too long. I never let my meetings go on for that long, and I should have shut him down twenty minutes earlier, but I was amusing myself with how talking about his wife turned his face the color of a firetruck.

The moment he held the paper back out to me, I yanked it out of his hand, and walked away. Slipping the paper into my pocket, I walked out of the bar and back into the alley.

As I strolled toward my downtown apartment, I couldn't help but chuckle. How big of an idiot was he to give the security code to get into his home to a known killer? It was then that I decided that I would definitely pay them a visit—*before* he left for his trip. Since I had the keys to the castle, I may as well have a little bit of fun.

CHAPTER 3

The Survivor

The closer I got to home, the tighter my chest became, threatening to squeeze out the air in my lungs. Although I knew it was stupid to return home, and that some would blame me for the bruises on my skin barely camouflaged by expensive makeup, leaving Joshua wasn't as simple as it seemed. Everything I had was tied to my husband's business. Our home. Our money. My business. Everything. Even if I were willing to throw it all away, the threats—and his connections—kept me at home. They made it impossible for me to escape him. Since my husband was more concerned about his public image than he was about me, he would not be willing to face the embarrassment of me leaving him. I was trapped in a life I didn't want and powerless to change it. The feeling that I had no control over my life and was completely powerless over it was overwhelming for me, but I didn't know what else to do.

Bane, the man who'd talked to me about the adventures of *Treasure Island* that morning, had never come to the register for his coffee. He must have slipped out when I returned behind the counter to fix it for him. It occupied my thoughts for the rest of the day. I couldn't fathom why he left a perfectly tasty, free cup of coffee on the counter. Even though I was married, I couldn't get him out of my mind, and it was troubling. His eyes had captivated me and held me in place until I didn't know which direction I was going. The fact that I would probably never see him again was for the best but fantasizing about him wasn't a bad thing. In a life overshadowed with darkness, the thought of the handsome stranger could bring in a little light.

The interstate traffic crawled along at a glacial place as I made my way through downtown, my mind keeping me occupied the entire time. The New Orleans freeways had been undergoing road construction for at least two decades, and I could see no end in sight. Even though I had left shortly after my store closed, the time of day didn't matter. There was always traffic.

Blowing out a breath, I pressed the key fob button to open the gate into my neighborhood, hoping my husband wasn't home. In the event he wasn't there, I could only speculate where he was, but anywhere was better than at home with me. I wasn't certain he had a mistress, but I wasn't naive either. A huge part of me hoped he had someone else. I hoped one day he would leave me for her, so I could move on with my life. Perhaps one day I would be able to build a family and experience true love. Until then, my secret IUD would remain in place. In no way would I bring a child into a loveless marriage. If I did, I would never be able to escape.

The night sky was dark when I pulled into the driveway, the lights of the city blotting out the stars. It was like as a visual representation of my life, the light in me nearly snuffed out by the constant barrage of suffering.

While the engine was still running, I sat in my car for a moment, not opening the garage door right away. If my husband was home, he would demand to know why I hadn't returned home the night before, and no excuse would suffice. He would accuse me of cheating, as he always did, and then we would fight all night long. Despite my better judgment, I had never cheated. I had never given myself the chance to feel pleasure without pain, but that didn't matter. He was a narcissist, a master of gaslighting, and I couldn't even remember how or when exactly he became that way. It was impossible for me to pinpoint the moment when my love had turned into a monster. He hadn't always been like that, but perhaps I had been so blinded by the good times that I had ignored all the warning signs. In any case, it didn't matter anymore. There was a lot I wished I could do over, but time only moved in one direction.

Swallowing down the fear that bubbled in my throat, I pressed the button to open my garage door. The moment I noticed my husband standing where I usually parked, with a glass of whiskey in his hand, my heart sank. His expression gave no indication of his mood, so I could not tell whether he was angry. Blood roared in my ears as my heart beat violently, my fight-or-flight instincts telling me to turn around and drive away. Still, I smiled at him—faked the happiest smile I could—as I slowly inched my vehicle into my space when he moved out of the way.

As soon as I shifted the car into park, he grabbed me by the arm and yanked me out of the car. One arm still ensnared in the seatbelt, I hit the concrete floor with a heavy thud. My hip and back exploded with pain just as the liquor glass hit the ground beside me, covering me with tiny glass shards. I cried out, tears burning the backs of my eyes, but he didn't give me a chance to process what was happening before he yanked me up by my shoulders and threw me up against the side of my car.

"Where the hell were you last night, Scarlett?" His voice was filled with vitriol, and the smell of whiskey on his breath nearly made me vomit. I tried to slow my breathing even as my body screamed in pain, but I knew he could see the fear in my eyes. I was nothing more than prey, a scared animal trapped in a cage.

"Josh, please calm down. While doing inventory at the bookstore, I fell asleep. It was—"

Surging forward, he grabbed my arm, his fingers digging into my flesh. "When I come home, I expect a hot meal waiting for me. Do you understand?"

I nodded, blinking back tears as I slid out of his grip and scurried into the house. Keeping my eyes downcast, I pulled leftovers out of the freezer, busying my hands preparing dinner. The kitchen was spotless, not a dish out of place. I had learned the hard way that a messy house only fueled Joshua's anger.

As I finished plating his food and set his plate on the table, my hands trembled. I stood motionless, watching him eat. My appetite was nonexistent.

After only a few bites, he slammed his fork down. "This chicken is dry. Can't you do anything right?"

Before I could respond, he grabbed the plate and flung it at me. I barely had time to duck as it shattered against the wall, shards of porcelain raining down around me as he rose from his chair.

"Useless bitch."

I scrambled backwards across the floor as he advanced, my back hitting the wall as he towered over me, his face contorted in rage. Curling into a ball, my arms did their best to shield my head when the first blow fell.

Over and over, his boot connected with my ribs, his fists punching me as I cried out in pain and pleaded for him to stop. After what felt like an eternity, he finally stepped back, breathing heavily.

"Clean up this mess," he spat, stalking out of the house. Only a second later, I heard him speed away, a sob of relief breaking free the moment he did.

Every inch of my body screamed in agony as I struggled to my hands and knees. I wanted to lie there and sob, but I knew better. Move, I told myself. *Survive.* This was not the first beating I had endured at Joshua's hands, and it likely wouldn't be the last. I refused to let him break me, but I couldn't leave. I couldn't even walk. For a moment, I just needed rest.

I dragged myself upstairs to my bathroom, barely able to stand. Leaning against the sink, I avoided my reflection in the mirror. I didn't need to see the damage to know it was bad. My ribs throbbed with every breath. When I lifted my shirt, dark bruises were already forming across my torso. My lip was split and bleeding, and my right eye was almost swollen shut.

Climbing into my bed, I finally allowed the tears to fall as I waited for the darkness to consume me and take the pain away.

CHAPTER 4
The Savior

"This should get you to the end of the month but let me know if you need more. I also ordered dinner. You need to eat."

Reaching into my pocket, I pulled out a brown envelope containing more than half of the cash I'd gotten earlier that day and handed it to my sister.

She narrowed her eyes at me, the expression making her look ten years younger and better rested. The past year had not been easy on Caroline. It hadn't been easy on any of us.

"Do I even need to ask?"

Turning to look at my seven-year-old niece in the hospital bed beside me, I shrugged but didn't answer. She and I both knew the envelope contained blood money—they always did. With a rare form of blood cancer ravaging Evelyn's body and the insurance not paying for the experimental treatment she was receiving, there were no other options. My sister lost her husband in a car accident and our parents were gone. They had no one else but me, and I would do anything to make sure they were taken care of.

"It doesn't matter where the money comes from, Cara. What matters is that Evie is taken care of and you don't have to leave her side or worry about working."

Even though her expression softened, I could still see the hesitation in her eyes. Stepping forward, I pulled her into a hug, my heart breaking when a sob burst from her throat. She was such a strong person, a fierce mother, but when I came to see them, my presence gave her permission to let go. I turned my attention to Evie, making sure she was still asleep, running my hand up and down my sister's back as she cried against my chest.

"They've kept her under all d-day." The weight of the day pressed down on her and bled into me, stuttering her words.

"Maybe they're just trying to make her sleep through the pain. She'll wake up again soon. The doctors know what they're doing."

Even if I didn't know what would happen, it was what we both wanted to be true, *needed* to be true. Trusting them was our only option.

I remained at the hospital until the moon was high in the sky, and visiting hours were long over.

After we'd eaten Chinese takeout, I watched over Evie as Caroline went home and showered, taking a little time for herself. She'd practically been living in the hospital ever since Evie had been admitted, and I knew it took a lot out of her. She needed that little escape.

Once I got back into my car, I pulled out my burner phone and contacted Phantom, the computer genius turned hacker, who was looking into the CEO who'd hired me that morning. He may have paid me to kill his wife, but I never went into a job without insurance, without knowing every single thing there was to know about my client. I didn't want to know the stuff that was already public. I wanted to know where his funds came from and where they went, who he was fucking and when, account numbers, back door affiliations...anything I could use against him if things went south.

While Phantom was still digging, he infiltrated the security code of the client's neighborhood gate and house, sending a signal to a wireless device in my pocket that would allow me entrance without incident. With free reign of his house and neighborhood, I pulled out of the hospital parking lot and headed toward the McMansion he called home.

Although I lived closer to downtown, I was familiar with the area the CEO lived in. The brick and wrought iron gate surrounded the entire neighborhood, giving its residents an illusion of safety that could be easily broken by a simple hack. When I arrived at the gate, I pulled my black hood over my head, merely holding the device up to my blacked-out window as I passed. The gate opened so quickly that I barely had to slow down.

Not wanting to park anywhere near his residence, I pulled my car into the driveway of another house, one that was listed for sale but not occupied.

Under the cover of darkness, my black clothes making me nothing more than a shadow, I made my way around the block, moving through backyards so I wouldn't show up on any cameras. The air was still, no noises but that of crickets and wildlife meeting my ears when I approached the back door of the CEO's home.

For several minutes I waited, peeking into the windows for any signs of movement. It was nearing midnight, but that didn't mean they weren't still awake.

Once I was sure no one was moving around inside the home, I pulled my lock-picking kit out of my pocket, the lock releasing quickly under my skilled maneuvering. The last thing I did before I opened the door was lift the device in my pocket again, making sure his security system was disarmed. Sure, he'd given me the access code, but I didn't want to chance it being the wrong numbers. He may have paid me, but I didn't trust him enough to believe he wouldn't try to trick me. I had my own methods, and they weren't to follow *his* directions.

Breaking into the opulent home was like taking candy from a baby. Once I was inside, I leaned against the wall nearest the garage, silently twisting the handle and peeking inside to see if they were even home. What I saw inside caught me by surprise. There was only one vehicle in the garage, a blue Lexus SUV, and the concrete beside it was covered in broken glass. Slipping through the open door, I closed it behind me, needing to take a closer look.

The smell of whiskey met my nose the moment I crouched beside the mess, telling me the glass was from someone's drink. What troubled me more was the drops of blood mixed within the shards. I silently cursed to myself, wondering what in the hell was going on in this man's home, and whether I'd led myself into a situation that was more trouble than it was worth. The only thing I did know was that he wasn't there, not if he was driving the silver BMW I'd seen him in earlier that day.

Leaving the garage behind, I crept up the staircase to the second level. If his wife was home, I expected her to be in the master bedroom. Since Phantom had already sent me pictures of the house's blueprints, I knew exactly where their bedroom was.

The double door entrance to the large suite was already open but the lights were off. I remained just outside for a moment, listening for any sounds coming from within, but there were none. If anyone was inside, they were asleep.

Blowing out a low breath, I pulled my mask over my face, and stepped into the room, making my way toward the bed. I didn't intend to kill her just yet, but I still wanted to see her before I made my way into her husband's office to see what he was hiding inside his safe.

Once I got close to the bed, however, my breath seized in my lungs, my body going stiff. His wife was the same woman I'd seen in the bookstore that morning, the stunning woman who'd chatted with me about books and had offered me a complimentary cup of coffee before I left. We'd only spoken for a few minutes, but I knew from that brief conversation that she was not the evil bitch he'd made her out to be. Usually I didn't care about those things, but by looking at her face, I got a better idea of why the garage was in the state it was in.

Rage burned inside of me, my hands squeezing into fists as it bubbled just below the surface. She wasn't asleep. She was unconscious, her beautiful face battered and bruised. Her eye was swollen shut and her lip was split. There were still glass shards in her arms and legs. He had beat her and left her like that, and he would fucking pay for it. She didn't deserve to die, and for some reason, that mattered to me.

I don't know why I did what I did next. Maybe it was because I'd spent hours with my sister and my niece before breaking into his house, or maybe it was some turn of fate forcing me to do the right thing, but instead of slicing her throat and finishing the job, I slid my hands beneath her body and pulled her into my arms. Her eyes never even opened as I carried her down the stairs and back outside, sticking to the shadows as I moved down the empty street, before setting her down gently on the backseat of my car.

Shifting my car into drive, I took her away from that house of horrors, my mission abandoned. All that mattered was getting her somewhere I could properly care for her wounds—and keep her hidden until I knew her husband wouldn't be able to have her killed by someone else. No one was going to lay a hand on her again...not if I had anything to say about it.

With my eyes on the unconscious form on the backseat of my car through the rearview mirror, I made my way through the darkened streets of New Orleans, heading toward my apartment. My mind raced, thoughts colliding as I tried to make sense of it all, but I had no hesitations. Just hours before, I'd been prepared to end the woman in the backseat's life. It was a job, nothing more. But seeing her battered and broken in that bed had shaken something loose inside me. My usual detached efficiency was gone, replaced by white-hot fury, and the primal need to protect.

She didn't stir as I carried her from the car to my bedroom, locked away in oblivion's refuge. Part of me was glad for that small mercy. It would spare her the pain, at least for the moment. Though her injuries turned my gut, I couldn't let it distract me. Even unconscious, she looked so small and vulnerable. It brought a familiar ache to my chest, reminding me of my niece in a way.

Once she was in my bed, I set to work tending her injuries, keeping my touch light. Bruises marred her pale skin, some older, some fresh and angry. My jaw clenched at the sight, but I tried to control my anger. As soon as I got hold of her husband, who I suspected was the person who had beaten her, I knew he would beg for death long before I granted it.

For the moment, I could only clean and dress her wounds with what supplies I had on hand. She needed a hospital, but that wasn't possible. Not until I understood why someone had wanted her dead—and who had nearly finished the job for me.

When the lines of pain eased from her beautiful face, she looked almost peaceful. I lingered at her bedside as she slept, a silent sentinel watching over her. Resolve hardened within me, absolute and unyielding. No matter what came next, I intended to keep her safe.

CHAPTER 5

The Survivor

*P*ain. Earth shattering pain consumed me when I awoke in a dark room, my head aching and cloudy. My left eye was swollen shut, affecting my vision, but I knew I was no longer in my home. It was the *only* thing I knew for sure.

"Hello?"

Nothing more than a croaked whisper escaped my lips when I tried to speak, but it had been enough to be heard outside the room. A moment later, the door creaked open and a large male silhouette moved into the open door-way—a silhouette I didn't recognize.

"Who are you? Where am I?"

Without a single word, he entered the room, my body instinctively pushing back on the bed as he approached me. As I watched his shadow as he got close enough for me to smell the scent of his shampoo, the lamp beside the bed flicked on. When the light brought his face into view, I was filled with more confusion than fear. After what I'd been through, I figured any man was safer than being with my husband, as crazy as that sounded. But the man in front of me was not who I would have expected to see.

Relief washed over me as memories came trickling back. I recalled strong arms lifting me, the rumble of an engine, the hypnotic streetlights flashing by as I drifted in and out of consciousness. Bane had saved me. He had brought me to his home, tended my wounds, but I didn't know why—or even how he knew where to find me.

"Bane? What's going on?"

Sitting in the chair next to the bed, the man from the bookstore held a glass of water toward me. I took it, my thirst overpowering my worry that he'd try to drug me. If he wanted to hurt me, he'd already had the perfect chance when I was unconscious.

"You don't need to be afraid. I'll explain everything, but you need rest right now. You probably have a concussion." He nudged the blanket aside with his hand, revealing the gauzy white bandages beneath. "There's no more glass in your skin and I've bandaged the worst of your wounds, but I imagine you'll be sore for a while."

It was then that I realized I was only wearing a bra and underwear. I pulled the blanket higher, my eyes never leaving his. "You're going to have to tell me more than that. Why am I with you? I don't even know you."

He huffed a chuckle, the sound sending a chill down my spine. "I think you may know *me* better than you know your own husband."

The words caused me to flinch just as much as the nonchalance in his tone. "What is that supposed to mean?"

Not answering right away, he grabbed a pill bottle off the side table and shook out a tablet, holding it out to me. When I didn't take it, he shrugged and set it aside. "You're with me because your husband paid me to kill you and I decided not to." He shrugged again, but the gesture looked forced, like there was a lot more he wasn't saying. If I was being honest, I wasn't sure I was ready to know. "From the way it looked to me, your husband was going to finish the job before anyone else ever got the chance."

Icy dread numbed my body from the chest down, my mind unable to process his claim, even though I knew everything he'd just said was the truth. Every day I spent with Joshua was like walking a tightrope. It was a realization I'd learned to live with. "Are you saying you went into my home to kill me, but you decided to..." I hesitated, the question bringing a bitter taste into my mouth. "You decided to do what—abduct me?"

Jaw clenching, Bane went quiet for several moments. As I waited for him to respond, my heart beat like a war drum against my ribcage, my airway tightening under the pressure.

Just when I thought I might climb out of my skin, he shook his head. "I didn't abduct you, Scarlett. I saved you, but I hadn't gone to your home to kill you. At least not yet."

Hearing that he had intended to kill me but then decided to save me only confused me more. My eyes darted around the room, searching for my clothes. I may have been in pain and my head was groggy, but I knew I needed to get away from him *and* my husband. I just needed to get...*away*. "Not yet? What would have convinced you to do it? Had I not been beaten? Is that why you came into my store? Were you stalking me?"

Before I had even finished my tirade, his head was already shaking, an exasperated look on his face. It took all the fight out of me and I slumped against the pillow, waiting for his response.

"Meeting you in the bookstore had been a complete co-incidence. I left the store quickly because I had to meet with your husband nearby. That was what brought me to the area in the first place. I had no idea that you were my next target when we'd spoken—"

"So, let me get this straight," I interrupted, his words sitting heavy in my stomach. "My husband met with you to plan my murder in a location right by my bookstore? He plotted to have his wife killed right where she'd poured her entire soul into creating her dream? Is that what you're telling me?"

This time, it was Bane who flinched, his light eyes going wide. I should have been petrified, and maybe it was because I was in shock, but I couldn't look away from him. This stranger had just told me he'd planned to kill me, and I was completely entranced by his face. Something was clearly wrong with me.

"Look," he started, leaning forward with his elbows on his knees, only bringing his face closer to mine. I couldn't blink as I hung on every word. "I did meet with your husband near your bookstore, and he did pay me to kill you as he rambled on about so much damn nonsense that I didn't even listen to. Usually, when I take a client, I don't care about their reasons why they want the person dead. So, I admittedly tuned out most of what he was saying."

Blowing out a breath, he leaned back in his chair, resting his ankle on his knee. "When I left that meeting, I got my people to dig into your husband, because something didn't sit right with me, and I needed insurance if I was going to follow through with his job. What I've discovered since that meeting, and even more once I brought you back here, is that there is a lot about your husband that you don't know. You're not safe with him. You'll only be safe if he thinks you're dead."

I studied his face. His icy blue eyes were tired but alert, scanning my injuries with clinical precision. Stubble darkened his hard jawline. Even bedraggled from watching over me, he exuded raw masculinity.

"How do you feel?" he asked, changing the subject as he dabbed at the gash on my forehead with antiseptic on a cloth. I winced as the alcohol met torn flesh.

"Sorry," he murmured. "Just cleaning it up."

His touch was uncharacteristically gentle. Bane, an assassin hardened by violence, transformed into a nurse before my eyes. It was...*unexpected*.

Shifting on the bed, I took stock of the dull ache in my ribs, the burn of the tiny cuts on my skin. "Sore. But better."

He nodded, reaching for fresh bandages. As he wrapped gauze around my wrist, his fingers grazed my skin, sending electricity into my very soul. His hands could end lives in a heartbeat, yet as they touched me, they held so much more.

"Your color's improving. With more rest, you'll heal quickly."

"Will I?" My voice wavered, my insecurities showing.

He met my gaze. "You're safe here, Little Red. I won't let anyone hurt you again."

I wanted to believe him, but my own husband had attacked me, and my savior was a contract killer. Nowhere was truly safe. Still, the determination in his eyes fortified me, so I managed a small smile.

"Thank you for taking care of me."

CHAPTER 6

The Savior

For the next several hours, I slept fitfully on my sofa, knowing my intended target was asleep in my bed, injured but alive. I didn't regret saving Scarlett, but I also didn't know what I would do with her. With her husband looking for someone to kill her, the last thing I could do was return her to her home. When I told her the best thing was for her husband to think she was dead, I wasn't being dramatic. It was true. Still, it hadn't been a well thought out plan, so I didn't know what my next steps should be. If I was a sane man, I would have left her with her husband and cut my losses, but I'd never been accused of being sane. I could have returned. She didn't need to be my responsibility, but after looking into her eyes, she'd somehow cast a spell on me, and I realized I couldn't have brought her back even if it killed me to keep her. If I were being honest, I knew it probably would.

Laying on my black leather sofa with my feet hanging off one side, I pulled out my phone and sent a message to Phantom. If I couldn't sleep, at least I could see if he had found new information. Now that I'd made keeping Scarlett safe my responsibility–something I was berating myself for–I would need more than just information. I would need somewhere to bring her where she wouldn't be found, and to possibly change her identity. No sooner had my message been sent than my phone rang.

"I'm not sure what your plan is, Boss, but you need to turn your television on right now. Local news channel."

Grunting my acknowledgment, I hung up the phone and reached for the remote, turning it to the channel he mentioned. The moment the feed started playing, my stomach dropped.

Fuck.

On the front steps of the police station stood Joshua Prejean looking every bit of a victim. Press cameras flashed in his face, his eyes bloodshot as though he'd been crying. I knew better than to buy it though.

"My beloved wife, Scarlett, was taken from our home last night while she was sleeping. If anyone has information about her whereabouts, please contact the police. Please bring my wife home to me."

Shaking my head, I ran my fingers through my hair. I should have known he would play the victim card, turning the entire situation into a spectacle. Seeing all I needed to see, I turned the television off just as the door to my bedroom clicked open, near-silent footsteps approaching me from behind.

Scarlett dragged her feet as she walked, the slide of her bare feet against the tile prickling my skin. With only her panties and one of my t-shirts on, which I'd given her as much for me as for her, she could have almost passed for my lover. However, no matter how stunning I thought she was, she was off limits. The way she looked dressed in my clothes, with my comforter wrapped around her petite body, gave my cock different ideas. It had been a long time since I'd had a woman in my bed, but Scarlett could not be that for me. The sooner I got her out of my life, the better.

I shifted on the sofa, sitting up and placing my phone on the coffee table.

"How much did you hear?"

The conflict coursing through her mind showed across her face as she stepped forward, lowering herself into the chair across from me. "What am I supposed to do? There's no way I can pretend to be dead. He's everywhere. I can't escape his reach."

After seeing some of the data Phantom had accumulated, I knew she was right about one thing. Her husband was everywhere, in government officials' pockets and connected to big money crime that extended far beyond New Orleans. There was one sure-fire way for her to escape him, however: if he was dead.

"I know your husband thinks he's the smartest guy in the room, and that his connections make him seem untouchable, but I am steps ahead of him."

The one thing I knew I had working for me was anonymity. Although I'd met her husband in the darkened corner of a hole-in-the-wall bar, I didn't think he could pick me out of a lineup. Not to mention, there was no way he would be able to point the finger at me, even if he did know my real name, without also implicating himself. I didn't know what his endgame was, but I had a feeling he was hoping her body would wash up on the banks of the Mississippi. In his mind, our deal was still on, and he was just waiting for me to follow through. Little did he know, my plans had changed.

As I sorted through the thoughts in my head, Scarlett sat quietly on the chair, her eyes scanning the room as her fingers played with the edges of the blanket. When I stood, intending to pour myself a glass of bourbon, she flinched, making me feel like utter shit. I may have been a killer, but I wasn't a woman beater. Crossing the room to my liquor cabinet, I poured two glasses, handing one to her as I sat back down. It was better that she didn't drink with pain medication in her system, but she needed a drink more than I did, and I hadn't given her enough to make her sick.

Checking my phone again, I scanned through some of the files Phantom had sent my way—files that included the police report her husband had already filled out that morning. "Your husband doesn't know my real identity, nor would he share it if he did. There's no way he could point the finger at me for taking you without explaining how I knew who you were or how I'd gotten past your security system. We'll stay put for the day so you can rest, and I can solidify our next move, but we will leave the city tonight. No matter your husband's reach, he won't be able to find you where we're going."

CHAPTER 7

The Survivor

Hearing my husband beg for my return was a shock to my senses, especially after what Bane had told me. Although I didn't know my abductor much better than I knew any stranger on the street, I knew my husband, and he was every bit as capable of doing something as heinous as ordering my death. I may not have trusted Bane, but I trusted Joshua even less. Still, I was conflicted. Sure, I'd thought of running before, leaving everything behind and starting over somewhere new, but I didn't want to lose everything I'd worked so hard for. I wanted to leave my marriage, but I didn't want to leave my shop, or my friends and family. Already, I knew Ashley would be worried sick, but I also knew she would take care of my store like it was her own.

Sitting in the chair across from Bane, in what I assumed was his apartment, I waited for him to tell me his plans. It seemed, however, as though he didn't have any. "I appreciate you choosing to, um..." Even as the words entered my mind, I shifted in my seat, unable to utter them out loud. "I appreciate you deciding to not kill me. I'm sure my husband was willing to pay you a hefty sum for it."

The way he chuckled rubbed me the wrong way, not that anything about my predicament was soothing to my soul. "Most intelligent people would know better than to pay an assassin in full before the deed is even done. I won't tell you what your life was worth, but it was worth *a lot.*"

The corner of his mouth lifted in a smirk, sending my stomach into a flutter. Something was clearly wrong with me, but I didn't have the mental capacity to analyze it yet. "To be honest, I'm not sure if I want to know."

Tossing back the rest of his bourbon, Bane stood, crossing the room to fill his glass. Mine still rested in my hand, no more than a sip missing. I couldn't help but to watch him as he moved around the space. He was nothing more than a shadow, dressed in black pants and a black short sleeved shirt that fit snugly to his muscular body. The only light that came from him came from his sky-blue eyes. They were a stark contrast to his dark hair and fringe of dark lashes.

"We'll need his money to keep you hidden until I can get close enough to him to take him out."

I should have been anticipating he would go after Josh, but his admission still caught me by surprise. An ache burrowed deep in my chest at the thought of my husband being killed, but I knew he didn't deserve to live. Still, no matter how evil he was, it was hard to think about him no longer existing in the world. "If my body never shows up, he will probably expect you to turn on him, if he doesn't already." I shifted in my seat again, anxiety and dread burning my chest. "Even if he dies, I just don't see how I'll ever be able to live a normal life again. Not in the city I was born and raised in."

Lowering himself back onto the sofa, Bane took a deep sip of his drink before setting it down on the coffee table. "It's certainly something to consider. I'm not concerned about his death coming back on you. You are innocent in this, and you will remain so. What I don't yet know is if you can return to the city once he's gone without going public about his abuse. It's certainly believable that an abused wife would go into hiding out of fear for her safety, but if you came back to the city after he's out of the picture, it could be perceived as too convenient. It would, however, make sense for you to leave and begin a new life elsewhere. We just must lay a trail for the police to find, revealing his illegal dealings enough to make it seem as though someone he'd screwed over got rid of him. A business transaction gone wrong... That's what the evidence *should* reveal."

As unsettled as I was, the concussion I'd suffered began to weigh down my eyelids the more we discussed plans to murder my husband. I wanted to stay awake, because sleeping only made me more vulnerable, but my body didn't agree. The topic was heavy, the details so much more than my conscience could balance with my morality.

Where I came from, murder was wrong, no matter what the person had done. What I was starting to realize the more time I spent with Bane, however, was that it wasn't always a black-and-white issue. He may have been an assassin, but his decision to spare me, to take my safety on as his responsibility, told me that he had a code, even if it was something he would never admit.

Pulling the blanket tighter around my body, I stood, the wounds on my thigh stinging with the motion. Bane's eyes tracked my movement, but he was silent until I'd nearly made it to the doorway of the bedroom. Before I disappeared back into the darkness, the sound of his footsteps drew my attention. When I looked over my shoulder, he was only a few steps away from me. It should have scared me to have him sneak up on me like that, but it didn't. I may have had a shitty survival instinct, but I wasn't afraid of him, although he was clearly a predator.

He stopped in front of the window, the sunlight lightening his eyes to near white as he peeked through the shades. "Get a few more hours of sleep. I'm going to get clothing for you brought here so you can get cleaned up before we leave and have everything you need. I want to leave the city by midnight."

CHAPTER 8

The Savior

After Scarlett went back to bed, I laid back on the sofa and dialed Phantom's number in my burner, but I didn't hit send right away. The way she flinched when I mentioned killing her husband had not escaped my notice. It wouldn't matter how she felt about it, because it was the only way to ensure her safety and freedom, but somehow I hoped she would have wanted it for herself. I hoped that in time she would, because I did not want to worry about her sharing my identity when she returned to her life and her conscience got the better of her. I didn't want to be forced to take her life after giving it back to her to protect my own. However, she and I both knew I would if she did something so stupid. There were very few people who knew who I was, and what I did for a living, and I could count them on one hand. She may not have known my real name, but she knew my face. She'd seen my apartment. That was enough to make me uncomfortable. I didn't regret my decision to save her, but I hoped I wouldn't start to. Protecting my identity at all costs was something I was determined to do, even if my conscience had found its way to the surface with her. Risking exposure—or worse, getting caught—was not an option.

Instead of sending the call to Phantom, realizing our conversation would go on for a while, I called my sister first. Scarlett needed clothing and other essentials to leave with me but taking her to a store would have been too risky.

Although I knew it bothered her, Caroline knew not to ask about the woman who was with me, or why I couldn't take her shopping for herself. In order to ensure her safety, my sister and I had an agreement that she would only know what she needed to know. I hated involving her at all, but she was the only person I trusted. She was the only solid person in my life—her and Evelyn.

If Scarlett hadn't been with me, I would have made my way to the hospital to see Evie, but even without me stopping by, I knew my sister needed a break. Anyone would find it difficult to sit in a hospital day in and day out, let alone watch their sick child unconscious in the bed. It would be good for her to let off some steam by going shopping, so I gave her a list for Scarlett, and gave her extra money for herself as well. It didn't matter if she grabbed a nice meal or got her nails done as long as she dropped everything off before nightfall. To be honest, I hoped she would treat herself. Caroline was worth every penny.

Once Caroline and I had finished our conversation, I called Phantom. Rather than a hello, my call was answered by him smacking on food and sucking loudly on a straw. The hacker may have been brilliant, but I was pretty sure he lived in his mother's basement, spending most of his time in a pair of white briefs and nothing else. "Are you done yet?" I asked, annoyance clear in my tone.

Taking another deep sip, the straw squelched as the well ran dry. "My apologies, Boss. Every now and then, I've got to eat. It takes nourishment for my brain to grow this big."

"The brain can't get much nutrition from a greasy drive-through burger." As though on cue, my stomach growled. Due to the events of the day, I couldn't even remember when I had eaten last. As tired as I was, and with so many things to do, it hadn't been my priority. "I'm chucking this phone today so make sure to answer when I call you from the new burner at midnight, maybe without slurping on a Big Gulp in my ear."

The sound of a wrapper being crumpled and tossed into a trashcan preceded another slurp of his straw in an empty cup. "Noted. What happens at midnight?"

Even when he knew I wouldn't disclose information, he never stopped asking. "It's a need-to-know basis, Phantom, and you don't need to know. Not yet, at least. Can you falsify dental records? Don't release them anywhere yet, just create them."

Before I finished the question, Phantom's fingers were already moving on his keyboard, the keystrokes so much faster than seemed humanly possible. I was pretty sure the guy could hack in his sleep. "I thought you had something challenging for me."

A chuckle escaped my lips. "That's not all. Do we know what our wannabe Mob boss is doing behind the scenes at the moment?"

A few more keystrokes made their way through the phone speaker. "Moving money from the joint accounts he shares with his wife into offshore accounts, small amounts at a time. He's been on his phone and his computer all day."

Standing from the sofa, I stepped into my office, opening my safe and loading up a duffel bag with money and documents for two fake identifications. "He thinks she ran. That's really good." I went quiet for a moment, double checking what I'd haphazardly thrown into the bag. Once I left my apartment, I wouldn't be back for a while. "Halt the transfers. I want to leave him guessing for a while. Right now, he's probably expecting her to return home."

I realized then that he might have believed she ran away rather than thought I killed her and hid her body a week before he wanted me to. It was something I could have used to my advantage.

"Got it. Anything else?"

I rubbed my eyes, trying to think as my body reminded me that it too needed rest. When I got off the phone,

I needed a quick nap before we headed to the cabin in the mountains of Alabama. A long drive lay ahead, and I couldn't drive if I was falling asleep. "Keep a record of any sums transferred to accounts that aren't his and fabricate eyewitness sightings of his wife west of Texas. I want to know who he is working with and I want him to think she's out there."

CHAPTER 9

The Survivor

The click of a door pulled me out of a deep sleep, the figure in the doorway causing me to blink a few times just to see if I was really seeing what I thought I was. After a moment, I remembered where I was, and who the half-naked man standing in the semi lit room was *my assassin.*

Bane stood in just inside the en suite bathroom, a fluffy white towel wrapped low on his hips as he brushed his teeth. For a moment, I just watched him as he brushed and flossed, not even realizing I was awake. His upper body was toned and cut with muscle, tattoos covering most of his back and at least one of his arms. From where I was laying, I couldn't make out what they were, but I had to admit, even to myself, that they only made him sexier. My CEO husband had no tattoos, nor was he in shape. Over the last few years, he'd really let himself go, drinking a lot more and putting on a lot of weight. My assassin savior couldn't have been more different.

Even though I knew it probably said something unfortunate about me, I secretly hoped the towel would fall. I'd never seen a man quite like him, and I knew nothing could ever happen between us, nor did I want it to. He wasn't the kind of man I would want to spend my life with, or have children with, but damn he was sexy.

When he turned to face the bedroom, however, I knew the fun was over, since he caught me ogling him. I expected him to shut the door and pull on some pants, but all he did was smirk before bending over to dig into one of the cabinets. He pulled out several items, tossing them into a toiletry bag, all with that cursed towel around his waist. The man was built like a god, making it impossible to look away.

"I'm finishing up here and then you can take a shower before we leave." With as much as he moved around as he spoke, I was surprised, and frankly disappointed, that the towel never loosened at all. It was almost like he'd added Velcro to it to keep it settled right above the money shot.

"My sister brought you some clothes and other things." Crossing the bedroom, he grabbed two large bags and set them on the foot of the bed. "Here you go. I hope you have everything here you'll need. If there's something else, just let me know and I'll see what I can do."

As he stepped into the large walk-in closet, I sat up and began digging into the bags. Inside one was a smaller bag filled with toiletries and products for women. There was shampoo, conditioner, and toothpaste, but also expensive face creams and toner, hair care products, tampons, and even a blow dryer. Most of the larger bags were filled with clothes, mostly black: tights, long shirts, night clothes, panties, and sports bras. I'd never met his sister, but it was clear she had a vague idea of what size I wore but chose looser fitting garments because she didn't want to risk buying anything that wouldn't fit. There were even a few pairs of shoes. I didn't know how long I would be with Bane, but from the looks of what his sister had bought for me, I realized I should be okay.

When Bane came back out of the closet, he was dressed in a fresh pair of black pants and a black shirt, a hoodie draped over his arm. "Don't tell me your closet is filled with twenty pairs of the exact same outfit."

He chuckled, sitting on the edge of the bed to pull on a pair of black boots. "There's probably a few other items in there, but I couldn't be sure since I don't wear them. Will the items in the bags work for you? Do you need anything else?"

My stomach growled, answering the question for me. "Your sister is amazing for finding all this stuff for me. Please tell her thank you."

The side of his mouth lifted in a half smile. "I'll do that, and I'll make something for us to eat. I want to hit the road soon so you should get your shower and get dressed."

Nodding, I reached back into the bags, taking out a pair of black joggers and a long black shirt. "Do you know where we're going? Is it a long way from here?"

He stood, tossing an empty duffle bag on the bed. "I do. We'll be driving most of the night. You can put your stuff in this. I'll give you some privacy and get something in the oven to eat. It won't be gourmet, but it's better than nothing."

Standing from the bed, I watched as he left the bedroom, shutting the door behind him. For a moment, I didn't move, clutching my new clothes close to my chest. The entire situation was surreal, and I should have been frightened. I kept reminding myself of that. But the more time I spent in Bane's company, the less I feared him. In my mind, I still knew what he was, but even though he was a villain, he didn't seem like a villain to me. He almost seemed like a hero.

Just like the rest of the apartment, Bane's en suite bathroom was upscale, sleek, and modern. The shower tile and the countertops were made of a shiny black stone, accented with flecks of metallic silver. The floor was also a polished stone, but in a light gray color. In the city of New Orleans, which was where I thought we were, based on what I could see out the window, the apartment was expensive. For an assassin, he must have been part of the upper echelon—if assassins had such a thing.

Once I took a shower and redressed my wounds, several of which were still painful, I put on my new clothes and went out to the kitchen. As I sat at the table eating a few slices of the pizza fresh from the oven, Bane finished packing everything he wanted to take, including boxes of food, and brought them out to his vehicle. By the items he was bringing to his car, it almost appeared as though we were going on vacation—a vacation where he would need to shoot and stab things. The sheer number of weapons he packed should have made me feel intimidated—something I'd thought repeatedly over the past day—but I didn't. If he'd wanted to hurt or kill me, he could have already, so I knew those weapons would not be used on me...at least I hoped they wouldn't. With any luck, I thought maybe he would teach me *how* to use them. One thing I'd never learned in life was self-defense, and after everything I'd been through, it was a skill I needed to learn. My life truly depended on it.

By the time I finished eating and took another pain pill, we climbed into Bane's car, a sleek, black Lexus with equally black tint on the windows, and left his apartment just before midnight. When we pulled out of the parking structure, I recognized the luxury apartment building. I'd never been inside it before Bane brought me there, but I had passed the building a few times.

"Is this level of window tint even legal?" I asked, trying to break the silence. Bane wasn't much of a talker, at least he didn't seem to be.

In the darkness, the smirk on his face was unmistakable. "Definitely not, but I've never been one to worry a whole lot about laws. If I did, I would make my money in a different way."

Reaching into the backseat, I grabbed a fleece blanket from our supplies and wrapped it around myself. Although I'd been sleeping for the better part of twenty-four hours, it was the middle of the night, so I intended to get comfortable enough to sleep through most of the drive.

"What city are we going to? Maybe I've been there."

Pressing a few buttons on the control panel, Bane selected a radio station that played grunge and alternative music, leaving the volume low. "We won't be staying in a city, not if we want the best chance of keeping you hidden."

The moment the answer left his lips, he turned the volume higher, signaling the end of our conversation.

For the next several hours, I dozed on and off, curled up with a blanket while Bane drove. The one thing I was grateful for was that he and I enjoyed the same genre of music. As dark as it was outside, I couldn't watch the sights outside the car window, not that there was anything to see. I'd driven that freeway north out of New Orleans many times, so I could have envisioned everything we passed in my mind anyway.

With the radio on and no conversation between us, my thoughts flipped like a picture book, from what had happened to me and my husband, to my shop, my friend, and how worried they would be, and back to the man sitting beside me. Even as his fingers tapped on the steering wheel to the music, he clenched his jaw often, making me wonder what was on his mind. I wasn't naive. I knew him saving me and taking on my safety as his responsibility put him and his entire way of life at risk. There was no question that he had done a huge favor for me. What I wanted to know was *why* he'd done it and what he was getting out of it. When we'd spoken in his living room, he'd explained some stuff, but he'd also left a lot unsaid.

Saving me and keeping the money my husband paid him to kill me would put him at odds with a very powerful man. Josh had an extensive network of people in high places, and from the few statements Bane had made, it seemed like my husband had more dangerous connections than even I knew about. While I appreciated him sparing me, I wanted to understand why he would do that when he knew the trouble it would cause for him. Maybe he *wanted* trouble with the people my husband associated with. Maybe he has a greater plan to dismantle the network my husband was a part of and that's why he did it. Without knowing the truth, without hearing it from his mouth, all I could do was speculate. Without knowing why he'd spared me, I would continue worrying that he would one day change his mind and kill me anyway.

CHAPTER 10

The Savior

Although Scarlett seemed more than willing to chat with me as I drove, I turned the volume up on the radio. We were not friends and I needed to make that clear, to her and to myself. The lifestyle I lived only worked if I kept everyone out of arm's reach, everyone except my sister and niece. Maybe one day that would change, and I would be ready for something more, but I wasn't there yet.

For the first few hours of the drive, my plan worked. Music blared from the car's speakers and Scarlett stared out the window at the darkness, or slept, neither of us uttering a word to the other. Halfway through Mississippi, however, she reached for the dial, nearly turning the music completely off.

"I know what you're doing." Even in the darkness, I could feel her eyes on the side of my face.

I shifted in my seat, glancing in my side view mirror to change lanes. "What's that?"

"You're avoiding me."

Huffing a chuckle, I flashed her a grin in an attempt to play it off. "Is that what I'm doing then? Would be kind of difficult, since you're sitting a foot away from me, Little Red."

She shrugged, turning to look out the window again. "You may be sitting next to me, but you couldn't be farther away."

The words trailed off at the end, but I hadn't missed them. It was clear that neither of us liked the idea of being vulnerable. I didn't respond for several beats, unsure of what to say. "I apologize if I'm making you uncomfortable. I'm not exactly a people-person." When I flashed another half-smile at her, she was watching me.

"You've certainly got the lone-wolf thing down."

Her feisty tone made me chuckle. "Well, damn. I thought I was better at hiding it. I *was* aiming more for mystery versus lone wolf, but I am kind of a wolf when you think about it."

In the corner of my eye, I saw the side of her mouth lift in a smile. "Do you choose to be a lone wolf or do others choose to stay away from you?"

Ouch. If I were being honest with myself, it was a little bit of both, but I would never admit that. "To be successful in my line of work, it's best to maintain my distance."

"Sounds lonely."

I shrugged. "I guess it would be for some, but I'm pretty used to it. I spend a lot of time with my sister and niece, so I'm not completely a hermit."

Her eyes lit up, her body turning to face me. "Tell me about them. You don't have to tell me their names or anything...just anything really."

I wished I hadn't mentioned my family. The last thing I wanted was to put my sister in any danger, but Scarlett already knew she existed since I'd told her about my sister buying her clothes. Not to mention, she didn't know my real name, so it wasn't like she could easily discover Caroline's identity. "It's been just me and my older sister for a long time. Well, us and my seven-year-old niece. The three of us are very close."

Instead of keeping the focus on me, I decided to turn the conversation back to her. "How about you tell me more about your husband and why he would want you dead so badly?"

Smile fading, she twisted back to look out the window, my question seeming to make her uncomfortable. "Are you insinuating that I must have done something to be worth killing me over?"

Shaking my head, I activated my turn signal as I moved to the exit lane to stop at a rest area to use the facilities. "I wasn't insinuating anything, nor did I say you deserved it. I'm just curious as to what you think his motives were."

I shrugged my shoulders, looking in my blind spot as I merged into the right lane. "I met with the guy and listened to him ramble for a good twenty minutes about why he wanted his wife dead. If I were being honest, I thought he was a half-crazed, narcissistic son of a bitch, who wanted to kill off his wife so he could marry his sidepiece. I was just curious how you saw it."

When she stiffened, I realized I may have been a little too brash in my explanation. The inside of the car went quiet for a few minutes, furthering that realization.

Parking the car outside the rest area, I turned to look at her, no longer expecting her to respond.

She cleared her throat, her eyes going distant. "My husband has been abusing me for a long time, physically, emotionally, verbally, and psychologically, but I thought I would never be free of him, because he was against divorce. He believes it would destroy his public image." Silencing my breaths, I hung on her next words, rage bubbling inside me again. "Until you took me from my home in the middle of the night and told me what my husband had hired you to do, I'd never known he was trying to have me killed." She huffed a cynical laugh. "Since he wasn't willing to get divorced, I guess killing me was his great 'plan b' for me. He would never be able to hold onto his wealth if he divorced me, not with who my father is."

I didn't think I'd ever wanted someone dead so much in my life.

CHAPTER II

The Survivor

After we stopped at a rest area to use the restroom, where Bane waited right outside the women's entrance while I was inside, we continued our journey in relative silence. It had surprised me when he told me about his sister and young niece, but it was also clear he didn't wish to talk about them. I got it. Although I wasn't a threat to them, I appreciated his need to keep them safe. He wasn't comfortable talking about his family and I didn't want to talk about my husband, so eventually I fell asleep. When I woke up again, it was to the sound of the car door opening.

Rubbing my eyes, I twisted my head, trying to ease the pinch in my neck from how I'd been sleeping. Bane stood beside the car, putting gas in it as he scanned the empty parking lot. I assumed he was worried we'd been followed, but I didn't ask. I had no idea where we were. The air outside was cooler, and the landscape, at least from what I could see, was no longer flat. One thing was for sure, we were nowhere near Louisiana.

When the gas pump clicked that it was finished, he poked his head back into the car, his light eyes nearly glowing in the fluorescent light. "Do you need to use the restroom or anything?"

I stretched, giving into my body's need to yawn. "How much longer do we have to go?"

Reaching into the car, he looked at his cellphone. "About forty-five minutes."

Outside my window, the sun was just beginning to rise above the horizon, highlighting the deep blue with oranges and pinks. "I could use some coffee, but I can wait until we get there."

By the look of the shadows under his eyes, it was clear he needed coffee and sleep, but I didn't say it out loud.

As we continued on in silence, I thought about my options. I knew I needed to stay away from Joshua, but that didn't mean I had to stay with the assassin who'd been hired to kill me either. I had no cash or identification, but if I could get away, I was sure there would be somewhere I could go to hide, somewhere I could have more control over my life. With Bane, I was completely at his mercy. So far, he'd been kind to me, but I didn't know if it was real, or if it would change. I didn't want to chance him turning on me or deciding I was more trouble than I was worth. The thought crushed something inside my chest, but I knew it was a possibility.

We got off the interstate again shortly after our pitstop in a town I'd never been to before. There were no businesses or homes near the exit, just mountains, trees, and more trees. It was a beautiful area, but completely rural.

"Are you taking me to the boonies?" I asked, humor in my tone. "Please tell me I won't have to use a porta-potty where we're going."

Letting out a chuckle, he turned a side eye to me. "The cabin is definitely in the sticks, but there is running water and basic amenities. I needed to keep you off the radar and I had just the place to do it. You'll be comfortable there."

By the time we pulled off the main road and onto a long rock-covered driveway, the sun had risen, sending streaks of light through the trees. We winded around the curvy path and then a small wooden cottage came into view. The structure was nestled among a cluster of tall pine trees, with a large porch and a brick chimney rising from the roof. The wood of the cottage had been weathered by time, the gray paint chipped and faded. There were a few other structures tucked away in the trees, one of which looked like a barn.

"Is this your place?"

The remoteness of the property made my chest tighten, anxiety of the unknown filling me with nervousness. I'd seen enough horror movies to make me imagine every scenario as I thought about sleeping in such a place.

Bypassing the driveway that led to the front of the house, Bane pulled around to the back, putting the car into park before turning in his seat to look at me. "Technically, yes, it is. It's a good place to escape to when you need to disappear for a while."

Although the outside of the cottage looked abandoned, the inside was cozy. It wasn't large, just a basic two-bedroom home with two bathrooms. However, the living area and kitchen were one open space, and the stone fireplace was a beautiful eye-catching feature.

While Bane unloaded the car, he insisted I sit on the sofa and rest. The injuries to my leg and arm ached, but not enough for me to listen. I stayed inside the cottage, but I unpacked everything as he brought it in, specifically the food items he'd boxed up. Surprisingly, the cabinets and freezer were already full.

The bedrooms were equal sized but one of them was clearly for Bane, since the closet was already filled with clothes, most of them black. When I'd picked on him for his lack of color before, I'd been borderline joking, but the moment I opened the closet in the cottage, I realized he was definitely obsessed with black everything. He didn't seem goth otherwise, but on my next visit to a store, I fully intended to buy him some black eyeliner. With his dark hair and bright eyes, I imagined it would actually make him sexier.

Ignoring all the thoughts about my assassin with a smoky eye, I grabbed the bag containing the items his sister bought for me and disappeared into the room that would be mine.

For a moment, I sat on the bed, smoothing my hands across the plush white comforter. The cottage walls were a sand color, but there were wooden beams accenting the walls and ceiling, giving it a rustic feel. The room itself was minimally furnished, with a queen bed, a dresser, and a five-shelf bookcase that was filled with books—mostly classics like 1984 and a collection of Edgar Allan Poe's short stories.

I stood, pulling a dusty copy of Fahrenheit 451 off the shelf and flipping through the worn pages. While I was there, I hoped to have time to read some of the books I'd yet to devour.

"Are you hungry?"

So, caught up in looking through the book collection, Bane's voice startled me. When I turned my head toward him, he was leaning against the doorframe, his hoodie abandoned. The short-sleeved black shirt fit his toned body like a glove.

"Is there coffee?"

He nodded, and as though on cue, the smell of coffee wafted through the air, luring me to follow behind the mysterious man in black when he turned and sauntered toward the kitchen.

"What's for breakfast?" I asked, watching the flex of his muscles from behind, realizing how inappropriate it was but not caring enough to stop.

Beating me to the coffee maker, he poured some in a surprisingly colorful mug and handed it to me before turning back to the stove. "I'm just throwing together an omelet. We'll eventually have to get more perishable food from the market," he said, cracking eggs into an already sizzling pan. "The creamer is in the refrigerator and the sugar is in the cabinet above the coffee maker. Help yourself."

After I fixed my coffee just the way I liked it and set it on the small table, I poured another mug for him and set it beside where he was working. I sat at the table while I waited for the food to be ready, not wanting to get in his way. It was odd to see him act so domesticated. Not much for words, Bane's actions said what his mouth didn't. He may have been a contract killer, but at the end of the day, he was just a regular guy. With the money he made taking lives, he had a family he loved and took care of, and a house he lived in and cooked in, just like everyone else. Well...not like everyone else, but it was what I had to tell myself so I didn't think about the stuff that would keep me up at night.

CHAPTER 12

The Savior

Bringing Scarlett to the cabin was the best decision to keep her safe, but it did have some drawbacks. One major issue was the cell service. The cellular service at the cottage was weak, but I did have Wi-Fi, so I mostly had to use Wi-Fi calling. Because of this, I tended to use my technology sparingly there. The other issue was the lack of entertainment. The cottage was on twenty private acres, so hiking was always an option, but there wasn't much to do inside the house aside from reading or playing board games. There was a television and a few Blu-ray videos, but there was no cable service. I knew it wouldn't take long before Scarlett went stir crazy being stuck in such small confines with me.

Something else that was weighing heavily on my mind was my next steps and how I was going to accomplish them. I never intended to just up and leave town with this woman forever, and I couldn't dispatch her husband from six hours away. At some point, I would have to find my way back to New Orleans if I was going to make the city safe for her once again. When I did return, I would have to figure out what to do with her.

After we ate breakfast, Scarlett offered to wash the dishes, but I insisted, needing to keep my head busy. Giving in quickly, she went into her bedroom, grabbing a book and then returning to the living room, where she curled up on the sofa to read. The book was Huckleberry Finn, one of my favorites.

When I finished washing the dishes, I grabbed my cell phone and walked outside, needing to call Phantom. Not having easy access to the local news was eating at me, but I knew he could fill me in on what was going on back home.

The covered deck on the back of the cottage was my favorite place to hang out, especially when it was raining. I loved watching storm clouds roll in, dumping torrential downpours, yet knowing they couldn't touch me. It was particularly chilly on this late autumn morning at the foot of the Appalachian Mountains, so I reminded myself I would need to bring wood back inside.

Dialing Phantom's number, I sat on one of the chairs on the deck, my legs stretched out in front of me. It only took one ring for him to answer.

"It's kind of early, Boss," he said, yawning a bit more dramatically than was necessary.

"Must be why I'm so tired."

It was then that I realized I hadn't slept in more than a day, aside from the few hours I got after I brought Scarlett to my home. When I got off the phone, I knew I would have to try to take a nap. I just hoped I could trust her not to get into trouble when I did.

Phantom cleared his throat. "So, what can I do for you on this lovely morning?"

Rubbing my hand down my face, I tried to remember why I'd called him in the first place. "Two things. I don't have great tech where I am, so I wanted to know if our guy has been making any other splashes on the news, and I wanted to know if he's been attempting to move around any more money."

In the background, Phantom's fingers flew across the keys, creating a cadence that nearly put me to sleep.

"The sighting in West Texas has been reported publicly, but they are also organizing a search of the swamps south of the city."

"Okay, that's good. If they're looking to the south and west, then they aren't looking here."

The hinges of the back door squealed as Scarlett opened it. Her gaze was hesitant, but I nodded, giving her permission to come outside although I was on a call. With the book in her hand, she walked across the deck and sat in the chair beside me, reopening the book on her lap. It took me a

98

moment to return to my conversation with Phantom as I watched her.

"Have they announced any suspects yet?"

Realizing I was talking about her, she closed the book and set it on her lap. I pulled the phone away from my ear and turned on the loudspeaker.

"No one has been announced yet," Phantom responded. "But the news channels have been parked outside her home since yesterday."

I nodded, searching her face. It was clear the revelation bothered her, but she remained silent. "And the money—has he moved anything else?"

Setting the book aside, she leaned forward in her chair. "Is he taking money from my trust? Or from my father's financial firm?"

Her question caught me by surprise. Up until that point, I hadn't asked her about her own family's money, not thinking it was relevant. I put the phone on the loudspeaker.

"Phantom, has he been tapping into her trust account or money from her father's financial firm?"

Keystrokes filled the space and Scarlett blew out a breath. "My father gave Joshua a loan to start his mortgage firm, but if Joshua divorces me, he would lose that resource. We both would. My trust only disperses to me if I'm married."

What Scarlett said caught me by surprise. "Your father based your entire trust on if you were married? What a guy."

Rolling her eyes, she leaned back in her chair. "Yeah. He's kind of a misogynistic piece of shit, to be honest. I guess I married my father."

I chuckled. I was so caught up talking to Scarlett, in how her dark eyes danced when she was being snarky, that I almost forgot I was on the phone until Phantom cleared his throat. "What you got, Phantom?"

"Alright. So. I will put a stop on Scarlett's trust right now, so he's been unable to pull anything from there. Since his accounts are frozen, it looks like he's tapped into another mortgage company, possibly a sister company. I would have to do more research to know more."

I stood from my chair, stretching my back. "Do that and get back to me later. Keep an eye on the search too. I want to know what he's doing."

"You got it, Boss."

After the call with Phantom, I went out to the woodshed and hauled some logs inside for the fireplace. The days were only going to get colder and the fireplace was able to heat much of the cottage effectively.

After lighting the fire, I fell asleep on the sofa as Scarlett curled up on the loveseat and read her book. I slept until late afternoon, grateful she was still there when I woke up. Part of me worried that she would take the first opportunity she could to run away, although she knew I was only trying to help her, and she'd agreed to let me. It was an unusual situation, and I still couldn't read her, so I didn't know what she was thinking. All I knew for sure–from the look on her face when I'd mentioned it–was that she wasn't comfortable with me killing her husband. Still, that was non-negotiable, so I was going to have to get her on board. Either that, or she would just have to deal with it, because I was going through with it anyway.

Sitting up on the sofa, I reached for my phone on the coffee table, checking to see if I'd missed any calls. Scarlett was still relaxed on the loveseat, her eyes barely open as though she'd either just woken up or she was about to fall asleep. When I stood up, however, her eyes tracked the movement.

"I'm glad you got some sleep," she said, closing her book. Dropping her feet onto the ground, she stretched her arms over her head. All I could think was how comfortable she looked curled up on the loveseat in her joggers, oversized sweatshirt, and thick white socks. I was glad to see it.

"Me too. I needed it." Grabbing another log, I tossed it onto the fire before heading toward the kitchen. "Do you want some coffee?"

The sound of her footsteps followed right behind me. "Absolutely. Do you need some help? I feel like a freeloader. You should at least let me make dinner or something."

I chuckled. "I won't complain if you cook a meal while we're here, but you're not a freeloader, so don't feel that way. I offered to bring you here and to keep you safe. In this cottage, I want you to make yourself at home. Cook if you want to cook. All I ask is that you talk to me before you go outside, because I need to know you're safe. Inside, you're safe. Once you go outside, you may not be."

CHAPTER 13

The Survivor

After Bane woke up from his nap on the sofa, we took our cups of coffee and returned to the chairs on the covered back deck. What was unexpected was the lazy Sunday feeling of sitting next to him, even under such extenuating circumstances. There was so much that should have been plaguing my mind—my store, my alleged disappearance, the fact that my husband was trying to steal all our money—but having no access to social media, or even my phone, was forcing me to put it to the back of my mind. I couldn't sit behind a screen and refresh repeatedly to see what was going on in my world. I knew that Bane's contact, Phantom, was keeping an eye on things for us, so that had to be enough for me.

"So," Bane started, turning his bright eyes in my direction. The midafternoon sky was overcast, making them appear nearly white. "I think we need to wait things out for a while. You're safe here, so there's no sense in bringing you back somewhere you won't be. Not until we get a better idea of what Joshua is going to do."

I nodded, setting my mug on the ground by my feet. "There has to be an end in sight, but I agree with you."

Dipping his head, he turned and looked out at the sky. I followed his line of sight, finally taking in the landscape. It truly was beautiful. Dense forests surrounded the cottage on all sides, mostly pine trees, but deciduous trees were scattered in between them. I breathed in deeply, taking in the fresh scent that was nothing like the scent of New Orleans. The city I lived in may have been a tourist trap, but it was a stinky one. "Is this all your land?"

He nodded, pointing toward the right where I could just barely see a mountain ridge over the trees. "I have twenty acres. My property line goes from that ridge and then follows the river on the south side of the property and the road on the other side."

The pride in his voice brought a smile to my face. My home was in a gated community and my yard was about five feet wide with no privacy. Although I always loved the idea of living somewhere with land and dimension, Josh never wanted to move away from the city. "This land is beautiful. I can see why you come here to get away. It smells good too. New Orleans kind of smells like piss and—"

"Vomit," he added, making me laugh.

"Yes. Oh, and car exhaust—especially in the downtown area. It's great."

When he chuckled, I was drawn to his mouth and how perfect it was, how straight and white his teeth were. It really was unfair that one person could be so attractive yet be so morally...*gray*. "Well, you won't find any of those smells here, except for maybe the vomit if you drink too much moonshine."

My eyes widened. "You know, I've never had moonshine before. Do you really have some here?" Although I knew drinking in his presence was probably a bad idea, I was under a lot of pressure, so maybe it was exactly what I needed. All I would have to do was not drink too much. *Easy*.

The look on his face was mischievous, his eyebrow arching. "I'm not so sure it would be a good idea for you to get into the moonshine, but yes, this is Alabama. I definitely have some."

Although his words said no, his face said maybe, so I decided to double down. "I've had a rough couple of days so how about we cook up food and then have some drinks while we play some board games or something. I mean, how drunk can I possibly get if my belly is full?"

"You really did think of everything."

With his apparent concession, or at least a loose one, I rose from my chair and returned inside. Digging through the refrigerator, I had a hard time narrowing down exactly what to cook for dinner. I knew Bane had brought an ice chest and a box of groceries, and there had already been food in the cottage's deep freezer and pantry when we'd gotten there, but we kind of looked like we were ready to film an episode of Doomsday Preppers. Since I was bound to a cabin in the middle of nowhere, I guessed it was fitting.

Approaching me from behind, he opened the freezer above me and pulled out a pack of frozen meat. "Do you want me to grill hamburgers?"

Just thinking about it made my stomach growl. Since Bane had slept through lunch, I'd only snacked on a bit of fruit and nuts throughout the day. "Absolutely."

My husband always expected me to stay thin, so he was very critical about what I ate. At that moment, I realized it would have been sweet justice if I returned to New Orleans twenty pounds heavier. Maybe I would even get Bane to teach me how to shoot a gun, become a completely different woman—a woman Joshua could never truly want.

For so many years I had walked on eggshells, a prisoner in my own skin, always afraid of what to say, what to eat, what to wear, of not being perfect. But with Bane, I didn't have to do that. I didn't know what there was between us—killer and victim, captive and savior—something different altogether. I didn't know, but I didn't think it needed a label. Regardless of what it was, I decided as I pulled out the rest of the ingredients for our burgers that I was going to just be myself and ride the wave. Even though I was legitimately hiding for my life, I hadn't felt so at peace—*so safe*—in a long time, and that said something about the state of my life. It was clear I was going through a metamorphosis and I was ready for every stage of that transformation. Bane, it seemed, would be the vehicle that would start the process of recovery and healing, as ironic as that was.

Since night had fallen and the air was too cold, Bane chose to cook our burgers on the stove instead of on an outdoor grill. While he worked on that, I washed the lettuce, sliced a tomato, pulled condiments out of the refrigerator, and plates out of the cabinet. We worked like a team, as crazy as that was. It was something Joshua and I never did. Although he'd agreed to let me have some of his moonshine after dinner, something I intended to hold him to, I brewed two cups of tea for our meal.

When the burgers were ready, we sat at the table together, the blaze in the fireplace warming the room and creating a feeling of camping. The thought made me stifle a laugh. "Maybe we should make s'mores one day."

Bane chuckled, taking a sip of his tea. "I haven't had s'mores in a long time. What made you think of them?"

Shrugging, I swallowed my food. I hadn't had a burger in ages, and it was cooked to perfection. "I was just thinking that this feels so much like camping. Well, more like glamping, so we should make smores."

Bane's chuckle turned into a bark of laughter, sending a flush to my cheeks. "Glamping?"

"Yes. Glamorous camping. It's a real thing. It's like camping. We're in the forest and eating grilled burgers. We'll play board games in front of a fire and drink moonshine, but we have real beds and a roof over our heads instead of sleeping in a tent. *Glamping.*"

Shaking his head, he continued to chuckle as he took a bite of his food, the firelight flickering in his eyes.

When he'd first taken me from my home and told me he'd been sent to kill me, I would have never thought he would be sitting across from me, eating a burger and laughing with me, but I wasn't complaining. I knew it wasn't going to last forever, and that the shoe would eventually drop, but until it did, I intended to just try to enjoy the respite. After years of pain, I deserved it.

Sitting across the table from Bane, my eyes lingered on the tattoos covering his muscular frame. Intricate, cryptic designs that hinted at hidden depths beneath his stoic exterior. I wondered what stories lurked in the ink etched into his skin.

Glancing up, he caught my stare. Although the flush across my cheeks deepened, I didn't look away. What I was doing was dangerous, but no more dangerous than living with an abusive sociopath.

"Do they hurt...the tattoos?"

His lips quirked up and he shrugged. "Sometimes. The pain reminds me I'm alive." He set his drink down and dipped his chin toward the bruises on my wrist. "And you?"

I tensed, pulling my sleeves down when old memories threatened to surface. Sensing my discomfort, he took my hand. His rough, calloused fingers entwined with mine. The contact anchored me, allowing the dark visions to recede.

"Another time. When you're ready, you can tell me about it."

Nodding, I squeezed his hand in silent gratitude. In the short time we'd known each other, Bane had proven himself a man of few words but profound empathy. He never pushed or pried, letting me set the pace of our blossoming connection.

I studied our entwined fingers, struck by the dichotomy. His hands could end lives in an instant, yet they cradled mine with exquisite tenderness, like a wild beast gently tamed.

"One day, you'll have to tell me about your tattoos." Letting go of his hand, I traced the intricate patterns of one of the designs on his arm, the swirls and shapes like nothing I'd ever seen before. They depicted scenes of violence and redemption, damnation and salvation. Each image told a story, but only he knew the full narrative etched into his flesh.

Although I kept expecting him to pull his arm away from me, he didn't, allowing me to run my fingers from one to another.

For a moment, I was completely entranced by this lethal man with a poet's soul. And though no more words passed between us while we finished dinner, and he never did tell me the story behind his tattoos, I'd never felt so deeply understood.

After dinner, Bane and I decided we would take showers and then watch a movie. I finished my shower first and returned to the living room, adding more wood to the fire and sitting on the sofa as I waited for him. The warm glow of the fireplace cast dancing shadows across the cabin walls, the events of the past few days replaying in my mind like a disturbing slideshow I couldn't turn off. I sat on the sofa, hugging my knees to my chest as I stared into the flickering flames.

Bane entered the room holding the first aid kit, sitting down beside me without a word. Lost in my own head, I tensed when he opened the kit and took my arm in his hand. His touch was gentle, caring, as he cleaned the gashes on my wrists with antiseptic wipes. I studied his face—the focused look in his piercing blue eyes, the furrow between his brows—and something stirred inside me. A man who kills for a living shouldn't be capable of such tenderness.

"This might sting a bit."

Biting my lip, I nodded, holding my breath until the stinging subsided as he spread ointment over my wounds. Once he was done, he wrapped my injuries with gauze, his fingers lingering for a moment after he secured the bandage. Our eyes met, the connection turning my cheeks warm. As a married woman, I knew it was wrong to feel anything for Bane, but I couldn't deny the spark that lingered just below the surface of my skin. I had no intention of acting on it, but it was there, nonetheless.

"Thank you."

Giving a slight nod, he moved to tend to the bruises on my face. I closed my eyes, unable to watch pity take shape on his features. His touch remained gentle, the brush of his fingers sending shivers skittering through my nerves like an electric charge that should never have been possible.

When he finished, he packed up the first aid kit and left the room to wash his hands. I stared after him, knowing I owed him more than I could ever repay, not just for rescuing me, but for treating me with a kindness I hadn't known in a long time. For the first time since Joshua's betrayal, I felt the faintest flicker of hope.

CHAPTER 14

The Savior

What surprised me the most as Scarlett and I prepared and ate dinner together was how willing she was to remain at the cottage with me for a while. I knew it was for the best. If we left her husband to stew, he would eventually show his hand. People like him couldn't handle not being in control. With his wife missing, and his financial accounts locked, he would eventually break. That would be when we would see him at his worst.

Finishing up our meal, we brought our plates to the kitchen. Scarlett insisted on cleaning up, as did I, so we settled on her washing the dishes, and me drying them and putting them away. It would have been comical to be behaving like an old married couple with this woman, if only she didn't have the ability to get my cock hard. I may have been the bad guy, but she was trouble.

"What game do you want to play?" she asked, excitement dancing in her dark eyes

I shrugged, leaning over to put the clean skillet back into the cabinet. "We could also watch a movie instead. I've got a few on Blu-ray. I'm pretty beat."

She shrugged, but I could tell she wasn't opposed to the idea. "What kind of movies do you have? I could maybe be swayed—as long as we play games one of these nights. I haven't had a game night in a long time."

Nodding, I tried to remember what videos I'd left at the cottage as I dried our plates. "I know I have a few horror flicks. I think I have The Shining and maybe some slasher movies."

Scarlett huffed a cynical laugh. "Well, that's fitting."

I scoffed, knocking my shoulder against hers. "I'm not a slasher. We can binge the Final Destination movies if you want. I think I have at least the first three here...but I can only handle one tonight."

With a laugh, she twisted to face me, turning off the faucet. "I'm definitely going to need a drink if we watch Final Destination, or I'll be expecting the entire house to kill me."

Once the kitchen was clean, Scarlett and I decided to put on our pajamas before curling up and watching a movie. It had been a long few days and we both wanted to freshen up and get comfortable. I didn't mind how much like a slumber party it felt. In my lifestyle, nights like this didn't usually happen, so I allowed myself to just relax and enjoy the moment for once.

Returning to my bedroom, I pulled on a pair of cotton pants and a sweatshirt and returned to the living room, adding more wood to the fire. Scarlett came out of her bedroom a few minutes later, wearing a set of purple fleece pajamas, her dark hair in waves flowing down her back.

"My sister did a good job getting you warm clothes for the climate, huh?"

She nodded as she smoothed out the hem of her shirt. "Yes. She really did an awesome job. She found a lot of stuff that fits me, even if it's a little big. I really hope you thank her for me."

To demonstrate, she pulled on the waistband of her pants, showing me that they were indeed a few sizes too big for her petite frame. The flash of the creamy skin of her flat stomach beneath made me have to suppress a groan. As wrong as it was, there was no doubt I would have to use my hand way more than I usually did while I was alone with her. She was a beautiful woman.

Pushing my twisted desires aside, I pulled a quilt out of a basket and handed it to her as she sat on the love seat, tucking her legs up beside her. "I'll definitely tell her. Do you really want moonshine?"

Although my gut instinct was for her not to drink, because I didn't want either of us to do something we would regret, I also wasn't going to be another man telling this strong woman what she could and couldn't do with her own body.

She scrunched her face, taking a moment to answer. "Do you have whiskey instead?"

I chuckled as I rose and crossed the room to the liquor cabinet. "I do."

Her smile pleased me more than it should have but I did my best to ignore my mind telling me how in trouble I was with her.

After half a glass of whiskey and thirty minutes of the movie, sleep found Scarlett just as easily as death found the dozen or so teenagers who'd tried cheating it.

Turning the movie off, I carried her into her bedroom, laying her down on the bed and covering her with the blankets. It was a cold night, so I left her door open when I walked back out, and then added more wood to the fire. As tired as I was, I intended to head straight to bed also, but when I picked up my cell phone from the coffee table, there were three missed calls from Phantom. *Fuck.*

Taking one more peek into Scarlett's room to make sure she was asleep, I went into my bedroom and shut the door. I would have preferred to talk on the phone outside to make sure she didn't overhear my conversation, but it had turned frigid overnight, and I didn't want to freeze my already blue balls off.

Once I was seated on my bed, I dialed the hacker's phone number. He answered on the first ring.

"Boss, we've got a problem."

The word sent my stomach into a tumble. I usually had nerves of steel, but there was so little I could control from where I was, and I didn't like it. "What?"

He went silent for a moment. "Did Scarlett tell you who her father is?"

My already tumbling stomach fell to the floor as I wondered if the woman I'd saved, who was sleeping in the bedroom next to me, was hiding something from me. "All she told me was that her father is in finance."

The way Phantom huffed a laugh did little to help my stress at that moment. "He's in finance all right. Bane, her father is Ivy Etienne."

The blood in my veins and the words on my tongue turned to ice, preventing me from speaking.

"Boss? Are you still there?"

It took me a few beats to respond, still trying to find my thoughts that had gotten away from me.

"Are you telling me that the woman I'm currently protecting is the daughter of one of the biggest Mob bosses in New Orleans?"

"That's what I'm telling you, but what I want to know is *why* did *she* not tell you?"

It was the same question I was asking myself and I didn't have an answer—unless she didn't know.

"In speaking to Scarlett, it doesn't sound like she has much of a relationship with her father. From what I know about him, he commits most of his crimes on the back of his businesses, so maybe she doesn't know about his Mob dealings, and believes he's just running a financial firm. She may be completely in the dark about how powerful and dangerous he is, just like she was in the dark about her husband. I don't think she's intentionally trying to hide it from me."

I knew it may have been merely wishful thinking, but at that second, it was the reasoning I was going with.

"So, are you going to ask her about it?"

"I'm not going to do anything just yet. I'm gonna wait things out and see if I can learn more about her relationship with her father first. I don't want to get on the bad side of his organization, but I am trying to protect his daughter and I'm sure he would want me to do just that. I will have to talk with him eventually, but I don't want to make any rash decisions."

Even as I said it, my mind whirled with how I needed to handle the situation. Nothing from my interactions with Scarlett made me believe she was being deceptive, but I needed her to come clean with me. I just didn't know how I was going to talk to her about her father, and I didn't know how I was going to talk to her father about her.

"Roger that, Boss. Anything else?"

Rubbing my hand over my eyes, exhaustion made it hard for me to think. "Keep your ears to the pavement for any movements or communications regarding Scarlett, her husband, or her father, and report back if you hear anything. I need to get some sleep. At least for a little while."

I hung up the phone a moment later, brushing my teeth and climbing into my bed. For a long while, thoughts warred my body for dominance, but my need for release was a physical entity in the room that I couldn't ignore.

Finally giving into the urge, I tossed my pants to the floor and slid my hand up my already rigid cock, my eyes rolling back at how fucking good it felt. With the frustrations of the past few days coursing through my system, I stroked myself harder, picking up the pace and closing my eyes as a reel played behind my eyelids. Images of a woman I should have not been envisioning at all flooded my mind without my permission, but the way she'd run her fingers across my tattoos, the way her eyes lit up when she laughed... it was impossible not to.

My breathing quickened, my orgasm approaching so much quicker than it usually did. I shuddered as my orgasm hit, ecstasy surging from my head to the tips of my toes as I tried to catch my breath between gasps, and all my thoughts centered around the one woman who shouldn't have been on my mind at all. But as I cleaned myself off and collapsed onto the bed, I couldn't find it in myself to care.

The rhythmic tapping of keys filled my ears as I pressed the phone closer. "Talk to me, Phantom. What have you got?"

"I'm in, Boss," he said between slurps and crunches. "Took some finesse, but Ivy's files are mine."

Shoving my feet into my boots, I headed out onto the deck. "Slow down and start from the beginning. What exactly did you uncover?"

Phantom let out an excited laugh. "Encrypted correspondence between Ivy and known crime syndicates across the city. Money transfers in untraceable crypto. Records of meetings and transactions that link him to every major player in the underground. And a hit ordered on Joshua Prejean. This is huge."

I stopped in my tracks, mind reeling. We knew Ivy had Mob ties, but confirmation brought a new edge to the danger Scarlett faced. If her own father was entangled in a web threatening her husband's life, nowhere was safe. Although I didn't know how her father was involved in the hit Joshua took out on Scarlett's life, her husband and father's business dealings were much too shady to not be a coincidence. And if her father wanted her husband dead...

"Send me everything," I said, resolve clear in my voice. "We need to get a better grasp of what's going on."

"Already on it." Keys clacked furiously through the phone as I hung up, my fists clenching at my sides, fury and focus coursing through me. Taking down Joshua was one thing, but Ivy raised the stakes. If it was a war they wanted, I'd bring hellfire to their doorsteps. For Scarlett, any cost was worth paying, but I didn't want her hurt in the process.

I paced as I waited for the files, thoughts racing. Scarlett had no idea the viper in her midst, the man who was supposed to love and protect her while plotting her husband's murder—the husband who was supposed to love and protect her while plotting *her* murder. Rage simmered in my blood, but underneath lay a shard of sorrow. However monstrous, Ivy was still her father. The betrayal would cut deep when the truth came to light. Joshua's betrayal had already hurt her enough, leaving wounds I wasn't sure would ever heal.

As my mind reeled, my phone chimed with an incoming message. I read Phantom's brief note then downloaded the encrypted attachment, entering my password with steady fingers. The archive opened, casting Ivy's sins in stark relief.

Emails arranging hits on Joshua's men, exchanges with Cartel leaders across the South, ledgers documenting payments for trafficking guns and drugs—the evidence was damning. Scarlett's name jumped out repeatedly, her movements tracked and reported. She was a pawn in their game, her life held cheap by all involved.

Jaw clenched, I forwarded the archive to my secure cloud storage. Ivy's days were numbered, but caution was critical with Scarlett in the crosshairs. I had to keep her away from New Orleans until the viper was defanged.

My phone rang again as I scrolled through everything in front of me, Phantom's concerned voice coming through when I answered with a grunt.

"What's the plan, Boss?"

I exhaled, my focus icy calm. "I'm going to keep her out of his reach while we tear their empire down."

CHAPTER 15
The Survivor

Still rubbing my eyes, I stumbled out of the bedroom when I woke to find Bane standing in the living room, already dressed for the day. We'd already been at the cottage for three days, most of which I'd spent either lounging, reading, or sleeping. Although I knew Bane spoke to Phantom often, checking on things back in New Orleans and plotting, I chose to remain ignorant for the most part. Ignorance truly was bliss. Instead, I'd finished reading *Huckleberry Finn* and had moved on to *The Catcher in the Rye*, which was a very different book, indeed.

With the fall weather cooling the air, we spent a lot of time on the deck, but in the evenings, we played games, mostly Life or Monopoly, which he totally let me cheat on. We'd also finished watching the first few Final Destination movies, so I was now too terrified to fly, drive, or ride a roller coaster. There was an ease about our interactions that I didn't want to question. It was something I would rather just enjoy because I realized it wouldn't last forever. Eventually, he would go back to his own life—which kept him on the other side of the law, and I would have to pick up the pieces and begin anew—something I didn't want to think about.

Although there was a sexual tension between us that bubbled just below the surface, at least for me, we were friends, or something like it, and it was exactly what I needed.

"How did you sleep?" he asked, closing his laptop. "I made coffee."

Before I'd answered the first question, he'd already turned around and headed into the kitchen. Smelling the coffee, I followed him. "I slept pretty well. Why are you so chipper this morning?"

When he turned around to hand me a cup of coffee, a grin was already tugging up the side of his mouth. "I don't think I've ever been accused of being chipper."

As in his usual fashion, Bane wore a black hoodie, but his cargo pants were a dark gray, which made me oddly proud.

Lifting the coffee pot, he poured more into his own cup, which was covered in cats in various poses. "It's a lovely day today, so I was thinking that, if your leg is feeling better, we could go on a hike. There's a place I would like to show you."

Living in South Louisiana, hiking in beautiful forests and mountains was not an option, so it wasn't something I ever got the chance to do, but some would have reminded me that Bane was a killer, friend or not. They would tell me I was crazy for even considering venturing into the forest with him, or being there with him at all, because what if he wanted to take me somewhere in the mountains to leave me for dead? But I knew that if he wanted me dead, he would have killed me already. If he wanted me dead, he wouldn't have been doing so much to take care of me. Maybe I was stupid. I didn't have the best track record with men, but I wasn't afraid of him. My instincts, no matter how misguided they were, told me I was safe.

"I'm not sure of my stamina, but we could certainly try. Are you going to tell me what you want to show me?"

The grin on his face was pure mischief as he grabbed a box of cereal. "Nope. It'll have to be a surprise."

After breakfast, Bane and I headed out on our walk. While I'd gotten ready, he'd prepared a fruit and sandwich lunch for us to bring with us. For an assassin, he was certainly in his element at the cottage, and he seemed glad to share it with someone else. I truly didn't know what to make of him. He was a complete enigma.

I was still surprised at how clear my head seemed, and I wondered if I could still be in shock. After being trapped under an abusive man's thumb for years, I couldn't deny that being away from him was freeing. But I also realized that the day would come when the reality of what I went through would hit me like a hurricane, and I would have to pick up the pieces and figure out where to go next.

The air outside was crisp, perfect for my jeans and hoodie, but the sun was shining bright, making me glad I had a short-sleeved shirt underneath, just in case I needed to shed the top layer.

Veering off the cottage's gravel driveway, I followed him as he ventured into the evergreen forest. Hiking down the roughly cleared trail, we were surrounded by a chaotic mixture of massive pine trees and deciduous trees that had begun losing their leaves for the upcoming winter. The air was thick and fragrant with the scent of pine needles and the earthy aroma of soil and moss. Sunlight filtered through the thick canopy of branches, creating dappled patterns on the forest floor. As the wind rustled the leaves, I breathed deeply, allowing the atmosphere to fill me with a peace I hadn't felt in a really long time.

I had to admit that as long as I'd lived in Louisiana, I'd always thought Alabama looked like the Gulf Coast, like the city of Mobile. Although I wasn't sure what city I was close to as I hiked up the mountain closest to Bane's cottage, the landscape looked absolutely *nothing* like Mobile. The mountains and trees were so much taller than I ever thought existed in such a southern state, and the fresh scent of the forest was pure joy.

For a good part of the hike, probably about an hour, I walked directly behind Bane, watching the black back- pack he wore that contained our lunch, water bottles, and hiking essentials bounce with each step, but eventually, the trail opened up, and I was able to walk by his side. He wasn't particularly chatty during the hike, which wasn't a bad thing, especially since I was used to living in a place below sea level and could barely catch my breath as we climbed in elevation. When I did ask him a question, he usually answered me, albeit with a brief response.

Every once in a while, I tried asking him personal ques- tions. Those were the questions with the vaguest re- sponses. It was clear he didn't want me to know a lot about his personal life. At least not anything past face value, which I understood. With his lifestyle, protecting his identity was important, but by this point, I kind of felt like we were in it together. Maybe he saw it differently. "Was the cottage a family home, or did you buy it as an adult?"

As I waited for his answer, he pulled a water bottle from the side pocket of the backpack and offered it to me. I took a sip and handed it back. I wasn't going to let him distract me.

When he put the water bottle back into the bag, he pulled out an apple and offered that to me as well. This time, however, he did not get one for himself.

"The cottage was not owned by my parents. What about you, Little Red? Do your parents own any vacation homes?"

I shined the apple on my sweatshirt, taking a bite and chewing before responding. "My parents are divorced, and I lived with my mom. My father paid child support and saw us sometimes, but he was more interested in buying our love than showing us love ... if that makes sense. So, I'm not really sure if he has vacation homes, but my mom did not, no. My grandparents on my mom's side had a fishing cabin down the bayou though."

His steps slowed as he turned around to face me, the grin on his face genuine. "Where down the bayou?"

Swallowing my apple, my cheeks heated at his intense interest. "Oh ... um ... Port Fourchon, I think. Somewhere between there and Grand Isle. I had a lot of fun there as a kid."

His grin only got wider but he spun around and started walking again. "Such a small world. I spent a lot of time there as a child as well, but I haven't been back often as an adult. Damn place gets torn to shreds every time there's a hurricane."

"I know! The news footage is always so disheartening. It would be nice to go back there one day though, just for the memories."

Walking beside me, he nodded. "Yeah. I've told my sister the same thing. One day, we will take my niece there and bring her fishing. With all the technology, kids don't get the same experiences as we did when I was a kid. I would love to change that for her."

I wasn't sure how long we'd talked when the forest finally opened up as we reached the top of the mountain, the sound of rushing water meeting my ears. Although I thought I could hear water as we walked, our conversation, and the wind through the dense foliage had all but drowned it out.

"Is that a—"

134

Bane stepped forward, a smile on his face as he held out his hand to pull me onto a large boulder. I hesitated for a moment, afraid I would slip off, but took a deep breath, and allowed him to help me climb up. Trusting him continued to get easier—trusting anyone really.

CHAPTER 16

The Savior

A bove the row of boulders on the ridge was a large waterfall that could only be seen at certain times of the year. Scarlett's dark eyes were bright with wonder as she took in the scene. The rapids from the falls made their way down the mountain until they joined the river below. I realized, as we watched the water crash against the rocks, that I would have to show her the river next. I also realized, as we talked during our hike, that she couldn't have known about her father's ties to organized crime. Over the past few days, as Phantom did more digging, I'd only skirted on the topic of family with Scarlett, not wanting to upset her. It became quite clear she didn't have a close relationship with her family, probably due to her abusive husband. The question was then, was I going to tell her about her father, and would she believe me? I wasn't sure of the answer to either question.

"This is breathtaking, Bane. Can we sit here, though? Because standing is kind of scaring the shit out of me."

Chuckling, I nodded. Still holding her by the arm, I guided her down until she was seated on the flat surface of the boulder, and then sat beside her, setting the backpack on the ground.

"This is the only time of the year that the flow of water is this strong, because the rains are heavy. It usually lasts for a few months, and then it freezes, but as it warms, the entire area behind us," I motioned to the clearing at the top of the ridge, "gets covered completely by different types of flowers, which draws thousands of butterflies. It's truly magical."

For a moment, she turned her gaze to me, her smile genuine and unbelievably breathtaking, but it was only for a moment. Something inside me shifted as I sat beside her, watching her as she watched the unrestrained, yet beautiful, waterfall. Somehow, this woman had poked holes in the carefully constructed, impenetrable walls I had built around myself for everyone except Caroline and Evelyn, and I wasn't sure what I thought about that. Either she was going to tear them down completely, creating a door to allow herself inside, or I was going to have to reinforce those walls and push her out. The thought of doing the latter, especially after all she'd been through, turned my stomach. I didn't think I could do it.

"I would love to see that."

So caught up in my head, I'd forgotten what we were talking about. "Sorry, my mind wandered. See what?"

Scarlett giggled, bumping my shoulder with hers. "The flowers and the butterflies. It must be amazing. When we walked through the forest, I kept expecting to see fairies, or gnomes, or something. It's just magical up here."

Gazing back at the tree line, I nodded. "Sometimes it's nice to at least pretend there's magic when you get out into the forest. It's one of the reasons I don't have much technology here. Well, that, and because I don't find the time to come here enough to make it worth it. When I am here, it forces me to get outside more."

Scarlett nodded, picking up a small piece of rock and twirling it in her hand. "It's good to unplug sometimes. Society is too dependent on technology. It has its benefits, but, at least for me, I wish I had the opportunity to get away to a place like this more often. For a bookstore owner, I don't read nearly enough books."

Although I grinned, the longing in her face made me want that for her too. "Maybe when this is all over, you'll be able to find something like this for yourself — some place you can go to when you need to get away from the city."

Silence fell between us for a while. In the corner of my eye, she took in the picturesque landscape, seeming to be deep in thought. I wondered if she was thinking about her husband, or if she was fully in the moment with me. That answer came a moment later when her smile fell, her eyes going distant.

"I never bothered planting flower beds at my home," she said, longing in her tone. "Although I always thought they were beautiful. It's just that..." Her voice trailed off as she plucked one of the few remaining wildflowers out of the ground and twirled it in her delicate fingers. "Most women love getting flowers from their spouses, but for me..."

A tear slid down her cheek and I couldn't help myself from wiping it away with my thumb. "What's wrong, Little Red? You know you can speak freely with me."

When she looked up to meet my gaze, there were so many unsaid words behind her eyes, yet all I wanted to do was kiss her, but I didn't dare.

To my relief, she looked away quickly, clearing her throat. "For me, flowers would show up as an apology—an apology for things I could never forgive, and things he would only do again. Maybe, one day, seeing them will bring me joy."

As the sun made its way toward the western horizon, Scarlett and I hiked down the mountain and back toward my
cottage. We'd spent a few hours near the waterfall, eating
lunch and talking, but the admission about Joshua's abuse
ceased after she told me he gave her flowers as apologies.
All it made me want to do was kill him more, but as long
as I was hours away and looking after her, my hands were
tied.

The conversation remained light-hearted after that. She
told me more about her childhood memories and favorite
things. I learned she loved working her way through the
banned books list, but her guilty pleasure was the genre of
smutty monster romances. Just the thought of such a thing
made me laugh, and it certainly gave me ammunition to
pick on her later. Although a reader myself, I had never
heard of such a thing.

The temperature dipped as late afternoon set in, threatening a cold night. Scarlett didn't have a coat, so I was glad
we got back to the cottage before nightfall. The last thing
I wanted was for her to get sick.

Dropping our hiking gear by the door, I crossed the room, stacking logs in the fireplace and setting it ablaze. She walked past me and stepped into the bathroom, shutting the door. I intended to go into the kitchen and plan dinner, but before I even had a chance to think about what I was going to do next, my cell phone vibrated in my pocket.

Pulling out the device, I recognized Phantom's number, so I answered it immediately. "Let me go outside."

I took one more glance at the bathroom door to make sure it was still closed, and then stepped outside, shutting the door behind me. Once I was on the deck, I sat down and then put the phone up to my ear. "What's up?"

"I've been worried about you, Boss. I've been calling you all day."

Although my phone had never rang, I wasn't surprised. Cellular service was hit or miss once too far away from the cottage.

"Sorry about that. We went on a hike. Cellular service is spotty. Is something going on?"

With a huff, Phantom's fingers tapped against the keyboard. "There's something I need you to see. Do you have your laptop with you? You may want to watch it on a larger screen than your phone and then tell me how you want to proceed."

It was clear by the tone of his voice that whatever he had to show me was a serious problem I would need to solve. After a relatively relaxing day, it was the last thing I needed. Even without knowing what it was about, a pit opened in my chest.

"Yeah. I have my laptop. Should I allow Scarlett to see whatever this is or not?"

Phantom went quiet for a moment, aside from the occasional keystroke. "If you want her to hate her husband more, then yes. Let her watch it. The encrypted file should be in your inbox now. I'll be waiting for further instructions."

CHAPTER 17

The Savior

F or several minutes, I remained on the deck, tapping my fingers on the arm of the chair as I watched the sunset over the ridge. There was no question that I wanted Scarlett to hate her husband—I wanted her to support me doing what I needed to do to ensure her safety and freedom moving forward, but I didn't want to see her hurt even more. Without knowing what was on the clip, I had no way to know if it would do more harm than good to her psyche.

As I thought, I went through the messages on my phone, deleting the four from Phantom, but hesitating when my finger landed on a message from my sister. I didn't have time to call her back at that moment, but the message said that Evie was having a good day with her treatments, so that was a sliver of good news to fill the darkness inside me. When things settled with the video, I would need to give Cara a call.

Blowing out a breath, I stood, making up my mind. If the video had something to do with Scarlett's husband, then I respected her enough not to keep it from her. Whatever it was, we would watch it together, and then we would deal with the fall out.

When I returned inside the cottage, Scarlett was in the kitchen, seasoning chicken she had laid out in a pan. The site of her preparing food for me turned my chest into complete mush. I grinned at her, but Phantom was waiting on my instructions, so I walked straight into my bedroom, opening the safe in my closet and pulling out my laptop.

Returning to the living room, I opened the laptop and set it on the coffee table. Scarlett was still in the kitchen, fully immersed in preparing dinner, but as the machine powered on, I approached her.

"What are you cooking? It looks amazing."

She looked up at me as she sliced a cucumber, a smile spreading across her lips.

"Baked chicken and a salad. There are a few boxes of pasta in the pantry though. I thought about throwing one of those together also."

After everything she'd gone through, her tenacity amazed me. She was a remarkable woman—a true phoenix.

"You didn't have to do all of this, especially after having such a long day."

With a shrug, she turned on the faucet and rinsed a tomato before setting it on the cutting board. "I don't mind. We have to eat, and it pays to keep myself busy."

Although I didn't say so, I understood completely. There were definitely things we had in common. As good as her mood was, I hated to ruin it, but I had no choice but to change the subject. Clearing my throat, I grabbed the decanter of whiskey and poured it into two glasses. "Phantom just sent an encrypted video to me. All I know is that it has something to do with your husband."

I turned to look at my laptop and then back at her, hating how her smile fell. "Are you able to step away from the food for a few minutes so we can see what this is all about?"

Opening the oven to peek at the food baking inside, she nodded. "I guess we should get it over with."

Hesitation still buzzed in my mind, but I turned around and led the way into the living area. With us both seated side-by-side on the sofa, I opened the encrypted file, taking a sip of my whiskey as I waited for it to load. The tension in the air was like a living entity in the room, Scarlett's posture was rigid, and her drink nearly gone.

The moment the video finished buffering, and the picture cleared, my hands curled into fists, rage already building.

On the front steps of his home, and surrounded by members of the press, Joshua Prejean stood behind a microphone in a press conference setting. I turned the volume louder on the laptop, unable to sit still.

"Have you heard from your wife?" one reporter, a middle-aged blond I recognized from one of the local news channels, asked.

"Have they found her body?" Another screamed from somewhere in the back, the question turning my stomach. As easy as I found it to take a life, I couldn't think about her that way, not with how I felt about her, whether or not I wanted to acknowledge it.

A few more questions were asked before Joshua's attorney lifted his hand to silence the crowd, the smug look on his face making me want to slice his throat and watch him bleed.

"Mr. Prejean has an update he would like to share," he said, his tone allowing no responses. "But you will hold off on your questions until he's finished saying what he needs to say."

Giving the press one more no-nonsense glare, the attorney moved to the side, and Joshua Prejean stepped forward.

"Here we go," Scarlett said in a deadpan tone, reaching for her whiskey glass and tossing the rest of it back.

Joshua cleared his throat. Although pain and betrayal showed on his face and deep shadows around his eyes indicated his lack of sleep, we both knew he was as full of shit as would be anything he was about to say.

The microphone crackled. "Up until last night, I grieved for my beloved wife, Scarlett. I thought someone had taken her in the night — had stolen her and hurt her. I've searched the swamps for her, cried for her, and prayed for her. Up until last night, I grieved for my wife. This morning, however, I discovered that the financial accounts I share with her have been frozen by someone other than myself. Money has been moved to other accounts. Without her body being found, and with a substantial amount of money from our shared accounts being stolen, I have reason to believe that my wife, Scarlett Prejean, is indeed alive and using *our* money to run away from our life together."

Dipping his head, Joshua pretended to wipe a tear away from his eyes. The living room in the cottage was dead silent.

A growl rumbled in my chest as I thought of all the ways I could murder him and make it look like a suicide, or a robbery. *Fuck*. At that moment, I just wanted him dead. I didn't care how it looked in the end, only that he suffered.

When he looked back at the camera, his eyes were glassy, but even I could tell it was fake. He was a bad actor.

"If something has happened to my beloved wife, and the perpetrator has stolen our money, please bring her home. But if it's you, Scarlett, and you're out there somewhere, then please come home. I love you, and I forgive you. We can still fix this."

CHAPTER 18

The Survivor

"**I**'m going to fucking kill him," Bane growled, slamming his hand down hard on the coffee table, making our glasses jingle.

I heard his words, but my brain was still trying to process what I'd just heard. I knew he was lying. I knew he was trying to manipulate me. It was just that... he was really good at it and it turned my stomach.

My fingers trembled as I twisted them into the hem of my thermal shirt. Next to me on the sofa, Bane's jaw was tense as he clicked out of the video, shutting down the laptop to get Joshua's face off the screen. I didn't need to watch it again.

The chime of the oven timer caught me by surprise, jolting me back into reality. I had almost forgotten I'd even set it. It was a good thing I had, because I would have definitely burned the chicken otherwise.

Bane looked at me as I stood up from the sofa, as though to say he could get whatever I needed, but I flashed him a small smile before turning on my heel and walking into the kitchen. Seeing Joshua call me a thief had been shocking, but I couldn't say I was truly surprised at that moment. I just needed to keep myself busy. If I didn't, I didn't know what else I would do.

Pulling the pan of chicken out of the oven, I set it on top of the stove and then turned the oven off.

For a stunted heartbeat, all I could do was lean my back against the counter, unsure what I was supposed to do. My biggest fear was that I was somehow breaking the law. Part of me knew it was my right to leave town, and that I hadn't actually taken any money, but Josh's public claims about me made me feel dirty...*stained*...like I could never be clean again.

Footprints approached the kitchen while my back was to the rest of the house, and when I looked up, Bane entered through the opened archway. Anger was no longer etched on his face. Instead, it had fallen into something more akin to concern, but sympathy was the last thing I wanted.

Moving away from the stove with my arms still wrapped around my middle, I dipped my chin toward the pan of chicken. "Dinner's ready."

Not giving the chicken a single glance, he took a step closer, reaching out his hand toward me. I flinched, making him pull back as though I'd burned him. "Scarlett, are you okay?"

For some reason, at that moment, I felt very vulnerable, and very defensive. I took a step back. "I'm fine. There's salad too if you're hungry."

The air in the cottage was too thin, and all I wanted to do was go outside, but the only way to get out was to go past Bane. I may not have been trapped, but at that moment, that was exactly how I felt—like a bird in a cage—and all I wanted was to fly. The problem was, my wings had been clipped a long time ago, and I didn't know how to grow them back.

Taking another step, he lifted his hand toward me again, but didn't touch me. In a way, I hoped he would. I needed to feel something—anything—other than what I was feeling, but I knew that was dangerous.

"Little Red, are you okay? It's going to be okay. Do you hear me? I'm not going to let him hurt you again. I'm not going to let anyone hurt you."

Still, I stared at his outstretched hand as though it was a viper, ready to strike. "What about you, Bane? It's your job to hurt people, isn't it? Are you not going to hurt me in the end?"

For a moment, he just stood there, neither of us saying anything, his hand not moving back, and mine not moving forward. The air was more charged than a lightning storm. Our eyes remained locked on each other, like a predator on their prey, and I knew the moment I turned away, he would attack. The problem was, I wasn't sure I didn't want him to. If anything, I was daring him to.

After a long bout of silence, he pulled his hand back toward his body, his jaw clenching. "No, Scarlett. I'm not going to hurt you. Hurting people may be my job, but I am not that person with you. I thought I'd shown you that already."

Huffing out a breath, he rubbed the scruff on his chin, gazing up at the ceiling. "Life would certainly be less complicated right now if I had treated you like I treat every other target, but I don't regret saving you, Scarlett. I don't regret it, and I don't know what this is." He motioned from himself, and then to me, sending my heart into the floor, its beat turning sluggish. "But this cannot go any further. I just need to keep you safe, that's all. Clearly I'm hurting you even when I'm trying not to."

With one more look into my eyes, he turned and walked away, his bedroom door closing behind him.

The moment the door closed, I slid down the wall, dropping to sit on the floor as my face crumpled into my hands. I knew the line Bane had drawn between us was for the best, but then why did it feel so wrong?

My chest threatened to implode, and all I wanted was for the ground beneath me to open up and swallow me whole. With everyone in New Orleans believing I'd run away from my picture-perfect life and stolen my husband's money, there was no way I could return there, even if Joshua did somehow disappear. With my luck, I would be blamed for that, too. The only way to possibly vindicate myself would be to prove my husband's abuse and shady business dealings, but I knew that was impossible. He had too many connections — too many people in his pocket. It would've been a classic case of he-said/she-said, and I knew I would lose.

When Bane and I had set off on our hike that morning, I'd wondered when the real pain would hit me — wondered if I was still in shock. As I curled up on the floor and the first sobbing wail ripped from my lips, I realized there was a lot I'd been holding back, even if I hadn't known it, and the dam was finally breaking.

I wasn't sure how long I'd been on the kitchen floor when I heard the click of a Bane's bedroom door, followed by his approaching footsteps. It could have been ten minutes, or it could've been hours, but I'd cried enough to dry out my eyes, and give myself a migraine. Even if I had things I needed to say to him at that moment, I no longer had the energy.

"Little Red." Crouching beside me, his fingers brushed the hair away from my face. "Are you okay? What can I do to help you? Just tell me how to make this better."

Shrugging, I closed my eyes as another tear slid down my cheek, my body numb.

Falling back on his heels, he looked toward the stove and then back at me. "Let me get this food put away, so it doesn't go bad after you've worked so hard on it, and then I'll get you to bed. Does that sound okay?"

All I could do was nod. I hated feeling so needy, but at that moment, I just really wanted someone to take care of me. Aside from Bane, I couldn't remember the last man who had – and that was saying something about my life.

Moving methodically around the kitchen, he placed the food I'd made into sealed containers, sneaking a few bites along the way. He offered some to me as well, but my appetite had left the moment I'd seen Joshua's face on the screen, painting me as a villain.

Once everything was in the refrigerator and the dishes were soaking in the sink, Bane returned to where I was still lying on the floor.

Crouching in front of me, he scooped me up into his arms like I weighed no more than a child and carried me to my bedroom, setting me down on the bed.

When he turned to walk away from me, I panicked and grabbed his hand. "Stay with me. *Please.*"

I'd never held his hand before, aside from that first night when I'd touched his tattoos, and I wasn't sure what had made me do it, but it seemed to catch him just as off guard as it had me.

"Scarlett, I ..."

Licking my lips, I closed my eyes, trying to think past my headache. "I have a migraine. It won't take me long to fall asleep. Please just stay with me until I do. I know it's a lot to ask but—"

"It's not." His thumb rubbed the top of my hand, as he sat in the chair next to the bed. "It's not too much to ask, but I just don't know if it's the best idea."

Even as he rejected me, I watched his hand in mine, desperate for him to stay. His hesitation hurt me more than he realized, more than I realized, but it wasn't something I could analyze, at least not yet.

"You said you would keep me safe, Bane, and I don't feel safe right now. I'm scared of what's going to happen now. That's why I'm asking you to stay. There is no other motive."

Blowing out a breath, he nodded, easing some of my panic. "I'll stay until you fall asleep but let me get you something for your headache."

CHAPTER 19

The Savior

The vibration of my phone in my pocket woke me from a deep sleep. I sat up, groaning as my aching back popped and cracked. It took me only a moment to realize, by the delicate hand lying only inches from mine, that I'd fallen asleep beside Scarlett's bed, crossing my own line in the sand.

Her response was the exact reason why I'd been hesitant to show her the video in the first place. After everything she'd been through, I never wanted to see her go through any more pain.

When she'd first tried to push me away in the kitchen, acting as though she wasn't safe in my presence, I'd gotten angry with her. I walked away. After only about ten minutes, however—after hearing the sounds of her pain—her heart wrenching sobs—that anger had melted away as though it had never been there. The anger was replaced by a desperate need to make her pain disappear. It was the reason I stayed with her until she fell asleep. What I hadn't counted on was falling asleep on the chair beside her bed.

With Scarlett still asleep, I slipped out of the bedroom and shut the door behind me. As I walked toward the door to the deck, I pulled my phone out of my pocket, picking up the pace when I noticed it was Caroline.

Lowering myself into one of the chairs, I answered the call. "Good morning." Although I hadn't checked the time, the brilliant sunrise told me it was early.

"Good morning to you." Just like the sunrise, my sister's voice was bright — happier than she'd sounded in weeks. "I have someone who wants to talk to you."

There was a slight crackle through the phone, and then a tiny voice, hoarse from being intubated, met my ears, immediately bringing tears to my eyes. "Good morning, Uncle Ethan! Guess what... Mommy got me a monkey. I named her Susie."

I chuckled, the smile on my face almost painful "Wow! I can't wait to meet her. Shall I get you another friend? Perhaps a puppy?"

Giggling, Evie pretended to think for a moment. "A puppy would be lovely, but I think I would also like a llama."

Even as I spoke to my niece on the phone, her innocent wit filling me with joy, I knew there were no guarantees with her health. It was a good sign that her doctors had woken her up, but that didn't mean they wouldn't put her to sleep again. Still, I treasured every moment I had with her, and I only regretted not being there to hug her and see her while she was awake. No matter what was happening with Scarlett, I would have to go to the hospital when I went back to the city. I needed to see the only family I had left.

"Well, I may need to go south of the border, little Evie, but I will bring you a llama."

There were hushed voices, and then Evie blew me an audible kiss through the phone, promising to see me later, alligator, before giving the phone back to her mother.

"Give me one second, E," Cara said, before pulling the phone away from her ear to speak with the nurse. I watched the horizon as I waited, the sky a beautiful clear blue with the sun just barely above the treetops.

"Okay, I'm back. The nurse is keeping her company while I run down to the cafeteria to grab breakfast," she said, the sounds of the intensive care unit fading as she walked.

"When did they wake her?"

"Early this morning. So far, her pain is tolerable. They've scheduled tests later this morning to check her levels. Hopefully, the meds are working." Caroline blew out a breath. "Hopefully, we can go home soon."

Once I finished the call with my sister, I sat on the deck for a while, knowing I needed to call Phantom, but trying to figure out a plan. I was torn. Part of me wanted to stay where we were for a while longer, because we were somewhere Scarlett was safe. The other part of me wanted to return to the city and deal with her husband before he caused any more trouble for her. Either way, when she woke up, I needed to have some semblance of a plan to lay out for her.

There was another option, one that had the potential to be the best-case scenario, but I didn't know how best to pull it off. The idea was to put Joshua Prejean at odds with Scarlett's father's mobster coalition—something to tip the scales. Ivy had already looked into having Joshua killed, but if he knew what Joshua had planned for her, that he'd hired an assassin to kill her, and if Ivy cared enough for his daughter to act, then I had little doubt her father would see to it that Joshua ended up at the bottom of the Mississippi. He certainly had the means to do it.

With a plan developing, I pulled my phone back out, dialing Phantom's phone number as I peeked in through the window to make sure Scarlett was still asleep.

As was always the case, the hacker answered quickly. "What's up, Boss? I thought I would hear back from you last night."

I grunted, not wanting to explain the drama that had unfolded after watching the video. "Watching the video was tough for her, but I think I have a plan."

Sucking very loudly on a straw, all I was able to make out was a mumbled acknowledgement.

"What we're going to do will have to be done with complete anonymity, and it must be untraceable. This cannot come back to us, and especially not to her."

Phantom huffed, feverishly typing on his keyboard. "This isn't amateur hour, Boss. Untraceable is my middle name."

"Funny... I figured it was something like Arthur, or possibly Winston."

In all honesty, I had no idea what Phantom's middle name was, or his first name, for that matter, but he'd probably already discovered mine. He was that good.

"Sorry to disappoint you, Boss, but my middle name is just not that cool. So... what do you need me to do?"

When I hung up with Phantom about twenty minutes later, my chest was noticeably tighter, but I knew our plan could work. All I had to do was wait until he sent me another video, hoping it would be the video we'd planned, and not another attempt from Joshua to manipulate the media into believing his narrative. If my plan worked, not only would it flip the script on him, turning the police's eyes on him instead of on Scarlett, but it would also make the crime lords of the city *very* interested in his affairs, seeking out their own version of justice for Ivy Etienne's daughter.

With the morning still clear and freezing temperatures coming that night, I made my way past the shed, grabbing an ax along the way so I could chop more wood. I would be showing Scarlett another video tonight that may stress her out, and we would be leaving the cottage sooner rather than later. The one thing she'd asked me to do was to make s'mores while we were still there, and I had every intention of making that happen for her tonight. There wasn't much I could control back in New Orleans, but I could keep her safe in our little spot in the rural Alabama woods, and

I could let her roast marshmallows for s'mores, so that's what I intended to do.

CHAPTER 20

The Survivor

Waking up the morning after my breakdown in the kitchen, I was hesitant to even leave my bedroom. My relationship with Bane, if I could even call it that, was complicated. He'd made it clear that nothing could ever develop between us, which was probably best, but I'd begged him to stay with me anyway. I'd held his hand, so I knew I'd crossed his line. As I slipped out of bed, still suffering from a headache, and got into the shower, I hoped he would pretend as though none of my vulnerability had ever broken through. I didn't know if I was ready to lay it all out in the open, even though I had in my moment of weakness.

When I finally left the bedroom, I wondered where I would find Bane and what I would say to him. As beautiful as the land around the cottage was, I wasn't surprised to find him outside. I was surprised to find him chopping wood without his shirt on, the sweat dripping down his sculpted torso drawing my attention directly to the tattoos that decorated his skin like a roadmap of his life. With the size of the wood pile, it was clear he'd been cutting for a while.

At first, I debated returning inside and not just standing there, ogling him like he was there for my viewing pleasure only, but I couldn't seem to help myself. Bane was undeniably a sexy man, but without a shirt, he was even more of a snack. Since I'd met him, he'd been covered head to toe in black, barely breaking that mold since we'd arrived at the cottage. In a way, I wondered if it was a part of his armor.

Lowering myself onto a chair, I opened my book on my lap. But, even as I tried to not to, I couldn't help but look at him. It didn't take long for me to forget about my neediness the night before. Since all good things came to an end, however, when Bane turned toward the cottage as he wiped his brow with a rag, his clear blue eyes landed right on mine, catching me red-handed.

I could've looked away and pretended I hadn't been watching him, but I realized that would have been more pathetic than just owning it. With a grin, I flipped the book closed, "Good morning. Have you been awake for a long time?"

Hacking the ax into a stump, he pulled his shirt back on as he walked toward me. "I've been up for about an hour. How did you sleep?'

When he made it onto the deck, he sat in the chair next to me, taking a sip of the water he'd left on the ground.

I shrugged, turning to look at the mountain ridge in the distance. The view was one I could look at every day and never get tired of it. "I've actually slept better here than I've slept in a long time. Last night was tough, but you helped make it better, so thank you."

A dip of his chin was his only response. For a moment after, things went quiet, only making my anxiety rev up my heart rate again.

Watching the trees sway in the wind, I waited for him to break the silence. It was clear he had something on his mind. He always did. But Bane was selective in what information he divulged and what he kept inside, so I knew when he was ready to talk, he would.

Spending so much time in the city, the stillness – the silence – of the air was almost nerving. It was like if I held my breath for too long, all hell would break loose. I really hoped that wasn't the case.

As though he felt the same way, he shifted beside me, setting his water on the ground and leaning back in his chair. "I spoke to Phantom this morning and we have a plan... but only time will tell if the plan will work."

With my eyes on his, I hung on every word, my chest tightening with every pause. I didn't dare speak, allowing him to continue.

"We need people to know the truth of what Joshua has done. We need the right people to know he hired someone to kill you and that he is one sleazy piece of shit. He's screwed a lot of people and going public could really help you."

Although I knew he was right, the idea of coming forward brought an unsettling heaviness to my chest. "If I come forward, won't that put me in more danger?"

Before I finished my statement, Bane was already shaking his head, which confused me more.

"You won't be coming forward anytime soon, Little Red. These aren't secrets you need to spill yourself."

The moment the words left his mouth, some of my fear dissipated, but my confusion didn't. "Then, how?"

"We will be making the accusations publicly, but completely anonymously. We don't need to prove anything to a court of law. We only need to sway public opinion and get the attention of those who may find his recent decisions enough of a reason to strap cement blocks to his shoes and throw him into the Mississippi."

I'd never heard of cement shoes anywhere except in Mob movies, so hearing it as a plan for my husband brought bile into the back of my throat, even if he was a monster. Although I knew Bane intended to kill Joshua, and although I realized more and more it was necessary, that didn't mean it was an easy pill to swallow. Evil or not, I'd spent years with Josh, and I had intended to spend many more with him, because I didn't see a way out. I was just tired of spending them in hell.

"Do you think there are people out there who would hunt him down if they knew — people who would kill him, so you don't have to?"

Something passed across his eyes – some truth he wasn't sharing — but it passed quickly.

I couldn't say for sure I wouldn't hold some resentment against Bane if he took Joshua's life. I knew that seemed silly. I realized Bane was a killer, but I had never seen him kill anyone, and I didn't know anyone he'd killed. If he took the life of my husband, however, it was something I didn't know I could forgive, and I didn't want that to come between us. I guessed, in some way, I cared about him too much to have Joshua's blood on his hands, no matter how many others he'd washed off.

With no hesitation on his face, he nodded. "I do think that will be the case, but I have to be prepared for any outcome. As of now, we will play this card. Phantom is getting a video together that will be fed onto local news channels during prime time later today. Then, we will wait a day or two so we can see what card Joshua plays in return, or if he has a chance to play one at all."

A cool breeze ruffled my hair as I looked at him, thinking more about how he'd held my hand as I had fallen asleep the night before, than thinking about my husband being killed. There was no love left between Joshua and me. I knew that, but it still hit my chest hard to admit to myself my marriage was over. I'd always thought I would be sad, but at that moment, I was numb more than anything else. Even in the numbness, however, there was an underlying excitement at the idea of finally being free.

"So, what do we do for now?"

Standing, Bane stretched his back. "We should probably go to the market, so we can get more food and the ingredients to make s'mores. Well...after I cover all the wood I seem to have chopped." He chuckled, his gaze turning to look at the enormous pile of wood still sitting outside the shed where he housed it to keep it dry. "Apparently, I got carried away."

CHAPTER 21

The Savior

After speaking to Phantom and my sister, I'd admittedly taken my frustrations out on several logs on my property. What I hadn't expected was the way Scarlett looked at me when she ventured onto the deck. The sooner we went our separate ways, the better. I knew that. But my need to be close to her was undeniable. In such a short period of time, I felt myself becoming addicted to her. She was like a drug, whether I wanted it or not.

Telling her about the plan had gone smoother than I'd expected, but I still couldn't find it in myself to tell her about her father. I really didn't think she knew the truth, and although I knew she would find out eventually, I didn't want to pile too much on her at once. Especially not after her breakdown the night before. Seeing Phantom's broadcast would be difficult enough for her.

When our conversation on the deck was finished, I moved the chopped wood into the woodshed, a task she insisted on helping me with. Only when I couldn't find another pair of gloves did I manage to talk her out of it. The warning of splinters and spider bites had been enough for her to stay on the deck while I worked. She was tough, but she was still healing.

Once the wood was put away, I slipped inside for a quick shower while she read her book. Afterwards, we returned outside together so we could head to the store.

Part of me knew it was a bad idea to take her anywhere, that once she was at the cabin, I needed to keep her out of sight, but we needed more food, and I didn't like the idea of leaving her alone. With the way her eyes had lit up at the mention of s'mores, I didn't want to let her down.

Instead of taking my car, since the last thing I wanted was to stand out in a town so small it had no stoplights, I pulled open the doors to the barn in the back of the property, revealing my father's old Chevy pickup truck. With limited parking in the city, I kept it at the cottage. It blended into the small town better than the big city anyway.

"You keep surprising me." Scarlett's smile was stunning as she circled the beat-up red truck, seeming to be in awe of the relic. "Is this so we will fit in? If so, then I think it's going to work."

Chuckling, I opened the passenger door for her, the hinges squealing and piercing the silent mountain air. "I'll be surprised if it starts up, but yes. That is the idea. Once I park my car in the barn and put the cover over it, I don't usually drive it again until I'm ready to leave town."

She nodded and slid onto the bench seat, closing the door behind her. "That makes sense. Are there a lot of people in this town who know you?"

Something I realized about Scarlett early on, was that she loved to dig for more information. Maybe that was the reader in her. I certainly couldn't blame her for trying, although there wasn't much I was willing to tell her that I hadn't already.

"The short answer would be no. It was why I bought a place in a town like this. When you escape to a random microscopic dot on a map, you're less likely to be found."

What I didn't bother saying out loud, because we both knew that no matter where we escaped to, there was always the chance of being found. When I pulled two baseball caps out from the glove compartment, popping one on my head and handing her the other, it was the one thought sitting stagnant in my mind. I hoped the old truck, old caps, and fishing gear in the back of the truck would make us look like nothing more than a local couple heading to the river to go fishing, but there was never any guarantee we wouldn't be recognized. Especially not when she was a missing person who was all over the news in New Orleans, as well as some of the national news channels.

Pulling up to the small, rundown market closest to my cottage, there were only two vehicles parked in the gravel parking lot. Both were covered in dust, as though they'd been driving on the unpaved roads and driveways common in the area. Nothing about either vehicle led me to think they were from out of town.

As I put the truck into park, I scanned the parking lot one more time, making sure there was no one lingering in either of the vehicles, or in the tree line surrounding the store. I already knew the store had no working security cameras, at least not from what I'd seen before, but if anything caught my eye that would put Scarlett at risk, I intended to put the truck back into gear and drive away. Everything, however, seemed to be calm outside the store. I was always on guard—always would be—but I was reasonably confident that our quick grocery stop wouldn't endanger her.

Powering off the engine, I turned to look at her. "Are you ready?" I had to admit the baseball cap on her head only made her more attractive. I kept reminding myself that the sooner we went our separate ways, the better, but the more I said it, the less I believed it. "Everything seems quiet outside the store, but we should get a game plan together."

Without waiting for her response, I opened the glove compartment and pulled out a small knife, handing it to her. Scarlett's eyes went wide, as though she was surprised I was giving her a weapon and wasn't sure if she should take it. After a moment of hesitation, she did, slipping it into her boot.

"Just in case something goes wrong, I want you to be able to protect yourself. You can keep that from now on."

She nodded, grazing her fingers over the sheath one more time, as though to make sure it was still there. "What about you?"

Lifting the hem of my shirt, I showed her the handgun and two knives attached to my waist. I never went anywhere unarmed, not if I could help it. "I'm going to leave the keys in the truck. If something goes wrong—if you need to get out of here, and for some reason I can't—I want you to take the truck and head back to the cottage. There is a safe room in the basement. That's where I'll find you."

The fear in her eyes tugged at something inside my chest. Before I could stop myself, before I could talk myself out of it, I reached for her hand, interlacing our fingers together. "You're going to be safe. I promise." Even as I said the words, I knew I was crossing the line again, but touching her was becoming more and more impossible to resist.

Her breath hitched as she watched our joint hands in the center of the seat between us. "Can we hold hands in the store… just so I don't have to worry about losing track of you?" The thought of holding her hand in a public place created a warmth in my chest that I didn't dare question.

With a nod, I opened the door and slid off the seat before reaching back in to help her to the ground. "That's not a bad idea, actually, it'll just further sell our story of being a couple going fishing."

Moving to stand by my side, she huffed a laugh as she slid her hand into mine again. "In that case, we should probably get some beer. You can't fish without beer."

Fifteen minutes later, we emerged from the store, fully stocked with the food items we needed, stuff to make s'mores, and lots of beer. To my relief, everything had gone without any issues. The cashier had seemed more interested in her cellphone than watching the store, and the second vehicle, an older model truck, belonged to an elderly man who was buying milk. It went so smoothly it almost felt like we were really shopping for a fishing trip, but I couldn't fool myself. That was why, instead of going straight back to the cottage when we left the store, I turned in the opposite direction. If anyone was watching us—following us—I intended to weed them out.

CHAPTER 22

The Survivor

Although Bane was confident we were safe entering the rural market to buy a few things, I wasn't surprised when he didn't go straight back to the cottage upon leaving the parking lot. Every decision he made showed me how significant my safety was to him, and I appreciated it more than he knew. As I sat beside him on the bench seat of the old Chevy pickup truck, I couldn't help but glance at him in his tattered red baseball cap with a college football logo on the front and see him as a regular guy. From the way he was with me and how he treated me, I couldn't imagine him as a killer. Deep down, I hoped that would never change.

When we got a few miles down the road, he took another look in the rearview mirror and then pulled into the gravel parking lot of a church. He drove the truck around the back of the building and parked it. The view behind the structure took my breath away. The river that flowed behind the church, running parallel to the road, was stunning, and the opposite bank was lined with dense forest just like the forest surrounding Bane's property.

"I think we're in the clear, but I figured we could sit here for a moment, just to make sure no one was following us," he said, turning the engine off and twisting in the seat to look at me, his sky blue eyes drawing me in. "Plus, I wanted to show you the river."

For a moment, all I could do was look at his face. I forgot for that moment how fucked up my life was, and how much danger I was truly in.

Eventually, he broke my stare, clearing his throat and reaching out to open the door. "Would you like to take a closer look?"

After another scan out the front windshield, I nodded. "Absolutely. It's beautiful here."

Bane opened the door, sliding out and then helping me to hop out beside him. The truck was much higher off the ground than I was used to.

Walking around the front of the truck, we stopped at a patch of grass on the edge of the riverbank. With the cool breeze, gentle flow of the water, and the fresh aroma of pine, I found myself in a state of tranquility I knew would never last.

"This river looks a lot cleaner than the Mississippi."

He chuckled, nodding his head as he crouched to pick up a few stones scattered across the grass.

"The Tennessee River is more than six hundred miles long, but some parts are dirtier than others."

I leaned forward, watching how the river snaked through the trees and mountains in both directions as far as I could see and all I wanted was to get into the water and explore. "You know something I've never done..." My train of thought trailed off as I watched Bane toss one of the stones into the water. It jumped three times before sinking beneath the surface.

"What have you never done?" he asked, crouching again to pick up a few more stones and then giving one to me. I tossed it, but without any of his skill, my stone sank immediately, sending the water around it rippling in gentle waves.

"I've never kayaked, but this looks like the perfect place to do it. It's so peaceful."

Handing me another stone, he moved closer to me. His scent, and the warmth of his body, sent shivers down my spine, settling right between my thighs. It was a dangerous feeling but one I didn't want to go away. If anything, I just really needed to masturbate. I needed the release.

"This part of the river is perfect for kayaking. When you're in a small craft, there are so many beautiful places to discover. Maybe one day, when this is all over, it'll be something you can experience."

The image his words painted for me made me smile. I only wished he would have offered to bring me himself. However, something told me that as soon as my circumstances improved, he would disappear from my life and I would never see him again. The thought twisted my gut, but I tried not to let it show on my face.

"Hopefully, I can start to enjoy my life. Maybe I can do all the living, laughing, and loving that I see printed on wall decor."

He chuckled again, launching another stone toward the water where it skipped multiple times before disappearing beneath the surface.

Looking at the stone still in my hand, I had no idea how he was getting it to do that. I turned to look at him. "Can you teach me how to make it jump like yours?"

Without hesitation, as though he was waiting for an invite, he moved even closer to me, wrapping his hand around mine. "That was exactly what I was about to do. Maybe learning to skip rocks and make s'mores can be the first step in your goal to live, laugh, love... Whatever that means."

Returning to the cottage an hour later, everything appeared to be as we'd left it, but Bane still wanted me to stay safely inside the locked truck as he checked the home for intruders.

Once he was sure it was secure, he returned to the truck and parked it back inside the barn where it could remain hidden. With all the forested land surrounding the property, there was still a prickle of unease on the back of my neck, telling me there could have been someone watching us, but I tried not to think about it. Even though our days thus far had been admittedly pleasant, especially considering the night we'd had before, I knew I wasn't on a getaway of any sort. I wasn't naïve, but the brief moments when I could let my guard down helped me handle all those moments when I couldn't.

Taking the grocery bags from the truck, I followed him back inside the cottage where we put everything away so we could prepare for our evening. He and Phantom had planned a news broadcast for that night that was sure to upset me just as much as the other had the night before.

Until then, however, we intended to grill steaks and make s'mores over the bonfire outside. I didn't know how much longer we were going to be at the cottage, but before we left the beautiful mountain retreat, I wanted to have at least one real camping experience.

Watching Bane prepare the meat, I was glad he was a good cook, because my husband never bothered. He seemed to know his way around ingredients and how to combine them into tasty dishes. It was one more thing about him that made him such a paradox—one more thing about him that disarmed me and made me see him as someone I wanted in my life.

The hiss of a bottle being opened met my ears just moments before Bane held out a beer out in front of me. "I assume since you asked for them that you wanted one, or do you want to wait until after dinner?"

With a grin, I took the bottle and swallowed back a deep swig. "If I wait to drink until after I eat, then I won't catch a buzz. I think I'll start now. How about you?"

Cocking an eyebrow, he pulled another bottle out of the refrigerator and popped the top off before taking a sip. "I'm going to go with you on this one. Although, I don't intend to drink more than one or two. I can't look after you if I'm drunk."

I snickered, taking another sip before setting my bottle on the counter so I could pull ingredients out of the refrigerator. "Don't you worry. I can look after myself tonight. You deserve a day off."

Although I knew it was a lie, since I wasn't all that capable of keeping myself safe, I just really wanted to see Bane cut loose a little. Ever since I'd met him, he'd always been so cautious—so on point—and he deserved to have a good time just as much as anyone else did.

For the next several minutes, Bane and I gathered everything we needed to make our meal and carried it all outside. While he worked on setting up the fire and getting the outdoor grill hot, I chopped some vegetables, threw together a fresh broccoli slaw, and put potatoes in the oven to bake. I did realize that, by the time we finished eating such a large meal, I may not even have enough space in my stomach to eat s'mores, but I fully intended to try.

CHAPTER 23

The Savior

While we prepared everything for our cookout, I could tell Scarlett's walls were lowered—that she seemed to feel safe. After crying to me the night before because she didn't, I was glad some of her fear had evaporated. However, I wasn't sure it was wise for her to let her guard down. The truth was, she *was* in danger, but at least for the night, I hoped to shoulder some of that weight for her. The smell of grilled meat filled the air as I flipped the steaks, the fire crackling in the background. For the moment, I was content to sit and enjoy the tranquil evening, savoring the moment with her.

Curled up in an Adirondack chair near the fire, Scarlett sipped a beer, watching as I cooked. Although I tried, I found it impossible not to look at her. Even in sweats and her long black hair pulled up in a messy bun, she was the most stunning woman I'd ever seen. She didn't need anything to make her more so.

As the sun disappeared behind the ridge, the sky was painted in brilliant shades of orange and pink, creating a beautiful backdrop. The evening air was chilly with the sun setting, causing Scarlett to bring out a blanket from the cottage.

"I don't even remember the last time I ate steak. It smells amazing."

I couldn't help but smile as she leaned forward in her chair, taking an exaggerated whiff of the meat cooking on the grill. The bruises that had yet to fully heal on her face infuriated me, but she truly was beautiful—inside and out. Like a light in the darkness, she had a contagious energy. It was inspiring to see how strong and resilient she was. She had been through so much, yet she still stood in the storm.

"You have been missing out. They're almost ready. Would you like to eat inside, or at the table on the deck?"

Setting the blanket aside, she stood, her dark eyes taking in the sunset before turning back to me. "Definitely outside. I will get everything else from the kitchen."

I nodded, watching as she walked away.

When the door closed behind her, I returned my attention to the grill, plating the meat and carrying it to the table. Even though the chicken she'd baked the night before was still in the refrigerator, I was glad we were eating outside in the fresh air after all the negative emotions she experienced in the kitchen the night before. With Phantom's broadcast hitting the news at any moment, I had no doubt the night would take a nosedive. Offering her an enjoyable meal in a serene setting was the least I could do to cushion the blow. All I had done all day was keep her distracted, but I realized we would eventually have to face reality again. I wasn't sure how she would react when Phantom and I followed through with a plan that would eventually lead to her husband's death. Furthermore, she still didn't know the truth about her father. There was a chance she would hate me when she found out that I knew and hadn't told her but breaking that news to her was something I continued to wrestle with. Still, I knew I had to do it. I just hoped she would understand.

Once we had everything set up on the outdoor table, Scarlett and I sat across from each other, trading in our beers for glasses of iced tea. Our conversation remained light, talking about our favorite things to do and her hopes and dreams for the future, how she hoped to return to her bookstore and maybe even open other branches. Her laugh was one of the most pleasing sounds I had ever heard. However, it was the little moans she made as she bit into her steak that made my cock stir—the sounds my body was convinced she made only for me. The last thing I wanted to do was seduce a woman who needed to heal, but the more time I spent with her, the more my body responded to her. I was like a moth to a flame, and I wasn't sure how long I could resist her.

Before we finished eating, my phone vibrated in my pocket, forcing me to step away from the table. With our plans for the evening, I wasn't surprised to see Phantom's phone number flashing across the screen.

With Scarlett still seated at the table, I returned to sit next to the fire, bringing the phone back to my ear. "Are we on?"

"We hacked into local news channels. The recording will be live in about an hour."

I glanced at Scarlett, who had stopped eating and was watching me, but she didn't move. "And the message?"

Phantom's fingers tapped across the keyboard as he spoke. "Let's put it this way, Boss. Once our message airs, the police won't be the only ones turning their attention to Joshua Prejean."

The moment I ended my conversation with Phantom, Scarlett rose from her chair. I didn't know if she would approach, so I grabbed a box of graham crackers for s'mores, making her smile.

"Do you have enough room in your belly for s'mores?" I asked, hoping my smile was reassuring. I may have been tense from our upcoming takeover of the news, but I didn't want her to be as well.

Instead of responding, she picked up the bag of marshmallows and impaled one on the wire. "Was that Phantom?"

I nodded, opening the chocolate as I watched her hold the marshmallow against the blaze, the flames reflecting in her dark eyes. "The recording will go live on the news in an hour. We don't catch New Orleans local news here, but he will send us a recording afterwards."

Her face was unreadable as she blew out the small fire on the tip of the marshmallow and held it toward me so I could sandwich it between the crackers and chocolate.

"Are you sure you want to watch it?" I asked, handing the s'more to her. "You don't have to."

The look in her eyes told me that my question caught her by surprise. I hated that I had to ask, but I didn't want to put her through more than she had already been through. Although I knew she wanted to know what was going on, I also realized that maybe it was best she didn't know everything—not if she wanted to rest easy at night.

Sliding the treat into her mouth, she closed her eyes, the groan she made telling me she enjoyed the taste nearly as much as she'd enjoyed the steak. It took everything in me to keep my mind on our discussion when her tongue licked the remaining marshmallow off her lips.

In my line of work, I didn't date, but I did scratch the itch when my hand wasn't enough. Spending so much time with Scarlett made it clear that when we went our separate ways, I would have to find a stranger who wanted nothing more than I did from the encounter. The problem was, after spending so much time with the woman next to me, I didn't know if a stranger would be enough. I wasn't sure if any woman could ever fill the jagged, gaping hole Scarlett would leave inside me when she walked out of my life.

The scary part was that I hadn't even kissed her yet. If I ever did, I knew my addiction to her would consume me. She would become everything to me, more than she already was, and I would destroy her. I hadn't chosen the name Bane as my alias for no reason. I chose it because I was destructive. She was much too good for me. She'd been damaged enough. In my head, I knew all those things, but I was still drawn to her like a magnet. If she had been any other target, I would have killed her without remorse. I wouldn't have left the state with her to keep her safe and thrown all the rules I'd lived by for years out of the window. It wasn't something I would have done for anyone else aside from the two remaining members of my family.

So caught up in my own thoughts as I watched the fire flicker, I hadn't even realized Scarlett was talking to me. Doing my best to clear my thoughts, I turned my eyes back to her. "I'm sorry. I zoned out for a minute."

She smiled, holding another marshmallow in front of me. "I said yes. I do want to watch the video. I'm tired of crying over Joshua. Whatever he's done to others and after what he's done to me... people should know the truth. I should know the truth.

Although I nodded, the fact that I was still keeping the truth from her about her father hadn't slipped my mind, and it made my stomach turn. It was another truth she deserved to know.

"You truly are one of the bravest people I know, Little Red. I just wanted you to know that." The way the fire lit up her face made it impossible for me to look away. "No matter what happens with Joshua, you'll be okay. I promise you that."

Her gaze turned to the fire, then back to me. A tear trailed down her cheek, telling me that she was still afraid, even if she didn't want to admit it.

Unable to help myself, which was becoming my excuse more and more, I leaned forward and wiped it away with my thumb. "What do I have to do to make you feel safe? Just tell m—"

"Stay with me," she said, cutting my question off mid-sentence.

When the words left her lips without hesitation, everything I knew—everything I'd been telling myself—went up in flames, disintegrating like ash in the air just like the walls I'd built up around myself. Without my permission, she'd knocked them all down.

Sliding my fingers into her hair, I closed the distance between us and kissed her, and when she opened for me, kissing me back, I knew I was lost.

CHAPTER 24

The Survivor

No matter how wrong it was—wrong for so many reasons—when Bane kissed me, every part of me needed to kiss him back. Even though I was married, and even though he was a man of *seriously* questionable morals, the moment his lips touched mine, there was no doubt in my heart that it was right.

The kiss was gentle at first—hesitant almost—his lips skating across mine as his fingers held me where he wanted me. But I needed so much more at that moment. So, when he went to pull away from me, I slanted my mouth over his to deepen the kiss, threading my fingers into his hair and bringing him closer.

The taste of him against my tongue sent ripples of pleasure through my body, making the neglected space between my thighs come alive after having been silent for so long. I knew I couldn't sleep with him. I couldn't take it that far, but damn I wanted to. I wanted him more than I'd ever wanted Joshua.

Sliding his arm around my waist, he pulled me closer until I was sitting on his lap, his need to be closer clearly as strong as my own.

"We shouldn't do this," he said, the words like blasphemy as he spoke them against my lips. Even as he said them, however, his mouth moved across mine like he couldn't stop either. A groan rumbled in his chest as he tasted me, the kiss turning more desperate.

"I know."

With no desire to move away, the words were weightless, escaping my lips in breaths against his skin at the same moment I trailed kisses from his mouth to his neck. "Do you want to stop? "Even though I asked the question, I already knew the answer. Neither of us wanted to stop.

Cupping the back of my head, he pulled my face toward his, his lips crashing against mine in a kiss that was filled with the same desperate need boiling inside of me. When he pulled away, he held my face only inches from his, forcing me to look into his clear blue eyes. "What I want doesn't matter, Little Red."

My heart pounded it as I tried to catch my breath, terrified of what he would say next, knowing I wouldn't be able to handle his rejection. He blew out a breath, leaning his forehead against mine. "When you're ready to be with someone again—when your wounds have healed—you'll find someone so much more worthy than I am."

I could never have anticipated how much his words would crush my heart. Years of abuse had not prepared me for the pain in my chest when he ran his fingers down my cheek and then looked away from me, guilt twisting his features as he stared at the fire.

For a moment, I lingered on his lap, not able to find the words to adequately express how I felt. In my head, I knew he was right, but I couldn't convince the rest of myself to move away from him. To the world, and even to himself, he was a villain. To me, however, he represented something so far removed from that. He'd sacrificed so much to save me when he had every reason not to. Not only had he saved me—a complete stranger who'd only crossed his path once in my bookstore—but he'd also placed a target on his own back by doing so. He'd been nothing but kind and generous to me. Even if he didn't think he was good enough—even if the world didn't think he was good enough—my heart disagreed.

Sliding my hand up his cheek, I tried to make him meet my gaze, but he resisted, a muscle clenching his jaw.

"Bane. *Please* just look at me. Let's talk about this."

With a slow shake of his head, he slid his arm around my waist and pulled me into a hug, kissing my forehead. The gesture sent an icy chill of rejection through my blood, and it took everything in me not to cry. All I wanted in life was to be free to make my own decisions, yet at that moment, I felt so fucking helpless. There was an open wound beneath my ribs, and I didn't know how to fix it. In mere moments, we'd gone from kissing with a fiery passion like I'd never experienced before, to him refusing to even look at me. The dramatic shift turned my stomach.

Loosening his hold on me, he nudged me to stand when his phone began to vibrate in his pocket.

"We should go inside," he said, pulling the device out without glancing at me, or at the screen. "That's probably Phantom calling. We have a video to watch."

When I rose from his lap and followed him inside, the pain and rejection was replaced by anxiety. Although he'd given me a good idea of what the recording was about, I didn't know the exact details. All I really knew was that Phantom had dirt on Joshua, and that particular dirt would cause people to doubt his claims about me and would also put him at odds with powerful people who were not opposed to taking the law into their own hands. There was also a very good chance whatever Phantom broadcasted would lead to Joshua's death, so I had to be okay with that. After all my husband had done to me, I was still not willing to pull the trigger myself, but after the claims he'd made about me on the news on top of everything else, I was becoming more and more comfortable with someone else doing it.

Closing the door behind us, Bane put his phone against his ear, only speaking to Phantom for a moment before hanging up. When he put his phone back into his pocket, he touched my arm, his face filled with things he wanted to say, but wouldn't.

"The broadcast went live thirty minutes ago. Phantom was able to keep it on the air for its entirety."

Even anticipating the update, my stomach still clinched at the confirmation, threatening to spill its contents on the floor.

"I'll go grab my laptop so we can watch it," he said, walking away from me.

I nodded, my hand resting on the back of the sofa as I watched him go into his bedroom. Without its support, I felt like I would collapse.

After disappearing into my own bedroom to use the bathroom, I went to the kitchen and poured a glass of whiskey for Bane and myself. We moved in a tense silence—him sitting on the sofa and logging into his laptop, and me pouring drinks and then sitting beside him. With the intimacy we'd shared by the fire, I wanted to touch him every second I watched him get everything ready. Just because he'd made his views about us going any further clear didn't mean I could turn everything off. There was something between us that neither of us could deny, no matter how hard he tried to claim he wasn't good enough.

"Are you ready for this?"

Bane's question pulled me out of my thoughts. Setting his glass down on the table, he turned to look at me, meeting my eyes as I stared at him without realizing it.

I nodded and took another sip of my drink, closing my eyes when the liquor burned its way down my throat. The truth was that I wasn't ready for any of what was happening to me, but it didn't matter. It all seemed to burn me in the end.

"Do we know what news channel it played on?" I asked, watching him navigate through screens.

Pulling his phone back out of his pocket, he flipped through the messages. "It looks like all of them—WDSU, WWLTV, FOX8, and WGNO for sure."

Dread burned the back of my throat when the realization hit me that everyone was finally seeing the truth about Joshua. I thought I was going to vomit but blew out a breath, doing my best to will the sensation away.

Setting my drink back down, I nodded and turned my eyes to the laptop's display. "Okay. I'm ready."

His finger hovered over the button for a few slow heartbeats. After a moment of staring at the still screen, he turned to look at me. It was clear there was something he wanted to say to me, but his hesitation only turned my stomach more.

"Bane? What's wrong? "I leaned back on the sofa, grabbing a throw pillow and holding it against my chest.

His eyes flicked back toward the laptop before returning to me again, only adding to my unease. He blew out a breath and I found myself taking it in. "Before we watch this, there are things you need to know."

CHAPTER 25

The Savior

As I sat beside Scarlett on the sofa, about to make her hate me for keeping secrets from her, all I could think about was our kiss by the fire. It had been a mistake. I knew that, but that didn't make me want her any less. But as badly as I wanted to kiss her again, I wanted what was in her best interest more, and that wasn't me. Pushing those thoughts to the back of my mind, I looked into her dark eyes, the worry on her face clear, and I hated myself for putting her through more shit.

"There are some things I would rather you hear from me than from someone else—especially from a broadcast."

She didn't even blink as she waited for me to continue, but the words were having a hard time finding their way out. Unable to stop myself, I reached for her hand. Even with everything I knew to be true, I didn't know how I would stay away from her. I didn't know if I was strong enough, or a good enough person.

"Did you know about Joshua's mistress?" Even as the words left my mouth, I berated myself for being a coward, and for not telling her about her father first.

Looking down at our hands, she nodded. "I knew he had them over the years, but I never knew the details. I never cared to know. He and I haven't had a spark in a long time."

Although I hated that she'd been in such an unhappy marriage, hearing she didn't desire him anymore warmed my frozen heart—as sick as that sounded. Joshua was truly a fool. I couldn't imagine a man wanting anyone other than her, but how I felt about her didn't matter. It was best for her if I let her go, so that was what I intended to do, but the reality of that decision was fucking crushing.

"When he hired me to get rid of you, he blabbed all about his current mistress, using her as a reason why he needed you dead."

Hearing the words come out of my own mouth threatened to make me sick, but I ignored my own reaction. Hers was the one that mattered. Scarlett's eyes blew wide, and she shifted on the sofa, pulling the blanket that was draped over the back down onto her lap. She was covering herself, trying to protect herself, and I hated that she felt the need to do so. All I wanted was to make her feel safe, but I was failing.

"I don't understand. He's had mistresses for years. Why is this one worth doing something so horrible to me?"

My chest tightened, knowing the blow I was about to drop on her. It was clear she didn't know the full truth, and I hated that I had to break it to her. I rubbed my thumb across the top of her hand, unsure of how to soothe her when he was the one who'd done her so wrong. "Because she was pregnant, Little Red. He said if he divorced you he would lose more money than you were worth. He wanted to be free to marry her... raise their child together."

For a moment, the air went silent between us. Then, without saying a word, she launched herself off the sofa and darted into her bedroom. Angry at myself for upsetting her, I followed, walking into the room just in time to hear her vomiting through the closed bathroom door. I tried to open it so I could help her, but it was locked.

"Scarlett, can you please let me in? Don't lock me out. "I leaned against the door, listening to her retch and hating that I'd done it to her. Sure, I wasn't the cheating piece of shit who had hurt her repeatedly, but maybe it would have been better for her not to know. "I'm going to get a cool rag for you."

Leaving her bedroom, I went into the kitchen, wetting a clean washcloth and bringing it back to her room. When I walked through the door, I was surprised to find her lying on the bed, curled up on her side.

Everything in me wanted to climb onto the bed and hold her, but I didn't. Instead, I walked around the other side and lowered myself into the chair I had fallen asleep in the night before. Her eyes opened to look up at me, but she didn't speak.

"Here," I said, reaching forward and wiping her face and neck with a damp washcloth. "This may help."

She closed her eyes, seeming to enjoy the coolness. "I'm sorry for upsetting you, Little Red. I never meant—"

"No." Opening her eyes, she reached out and grabbed my hand, stopping my ministrations. "Don't you dare take the blame for what *he* did to me. You didn't do anything wrong. He should have told me about her. I would have gladly let him go, but I'm not surprised he cared more about the money. *You* are not to blame in any of this. He is."

Although I knew she believed everything she said, I also knew I would continue to blame myself because I should've told her sooner. "He's a dirtbag and deserves everything that's coming to him." Setting the cloth aside, I used my other hand to brush the hair away from her face. Even after being sick, her beauty made my chest squeeze even tighter. "He won't get away with this, Scarlett, and once he's gone, you'll be able to go after everything you've ever wanted. No one will hold you back anymore."

When she looked away from me, her eyes going glassy, I realized my words hadn't landed the way I'd wanted them too. "What's wrong? Did I say something to upset you?"

Without looking at me, she squeezed her eyes shut and shook her head. When her eyes flicked back up to meet mine, a tear trailed down her cheek, destroying me from the inside. "You keep saying I can have whatever I want, Bane, but what if what I want is you?"

Rolling onto her back, she wrapped her arms around my waist and pulled me on top of her, pressing her lips to mine. My cock was as hard as steel, so there was no way she didn't feel it when I nestled between her thighs. There was no way for me to hide how much I desired her. The only thing keeping us apart and protecting her from me was our clothing, and that was incredibly dangerous. Although I'd promised myself that I wouldn't go any further than kissing her, it was clear she didn't intend to make it easy for me.

CHAPTER 26

The Survivor

A s Bane's hips settled between my thighs, everything else left my mind. I wanted him badly. My entire body begged to be touched by him—to have him inside of me. I needed it more than I needed air.

Pulling away from my lips, he rested his forehead against mine, both of us left panting, the kiss making me glad I'd brushed, and mouth washed before leaving the bathroom.

"I need you to understand we can't go any further than this right now. If you want to judge whether I'm good enough for you or not, I can accept that, but I'm not comfortable with moving too fast. There are too many unknowns right now, and you have been through so much already."

Even though I understood his words, they still hurt my chest. They still felt too much like rejection. He was more than just a distraction to me, but sex could be a perfect distraction, and it was exactly what I needed at that moment. Still, I had to take what I could get.

Lifting my mouth to his, I kissed him deeply, claiming him as mine, forcing a groan from his chest. When I pulled away, we were both breathless.

"I know you want to protect me, Bane, but I want you—all of you."

Closing his eyes, he threaded his fingers in my hair. "I know you do, Little Red. I want you too—more than you know—but we still have much to discuss, a video to watch, and a lot of really important shit to plan. If I slid inside of you tonight, we would spend the next week in this bed, because I would never be able to get enough, but all that would do is put you more in danger. I can't lose track of our reality right now—not if I want to protect you. When you're safe, I promise I'll make it up to you."

The hardline Bane drew in the sand was disappointing, but I understood why he did it. Still, my body was on fire, my pussy throbbing against his still clothed hardness between my legs, and I had a difficult time thinking about anything else.

"Do you still want to watch the video tonight? I don't feel sick anymore, so I think I can handle it."

Without responding, he wrapped his arms around me and rolled us over until he was on his back. The moment I was straddling him, I slid against the hard bar of him that was lined up against my center, only making me want him more. The heat he was packing was impressive.

Unable to help myself, I rolled my hips, dragging my pussy against his erection, cursing our clothes for being between us. A guttural moan rumbled out of him, telling me he enjoyed it, but he still grabbed my hips and halted my movement. "If you keep doing that, I will lose the fight I'm struggling to maintain my willpower."

My lips tipping up in a grin, I didn't bother telling him that was my plan, because he already knew it. "If you want me to stop, then we should probably get out of this bed because my willpower is already gone. What I really need is to come. It's been a long time."

The groan that came from him was more pained than an injured animal. Digging his fingers into my ass, he lifted his hips and dragged me against him, sending my eyes into the back of my head. "I won't fuck you yet, Little Red, because once I do, you'll be mine forever, but I didn't say anything about not being willing to make you come. If that's what you need to hold you over, then I'm sure I could help."

His words sent electric heat surging all the way down into my core, my pussy begging to be filled. "*Please*."

The minute the plea left my mouth, he flipped me back on my back, tugging on the waistline of my pants. "Take these off, so I can help you release some tension."

I giggled, sliding my pants and panties down and kicking them to the floor. "Is that what they're calling it?"

The smirk he shot at me was purely evil, but his eyes turned hungry when his gaze shifted to between my thighs, his tongue swiping across his lips. *Damn*. He was so fucking sexy.

"Are you sure you want me to touch you, Little Red? I don't want you to do anything you aren't ready for."

Opening my thighs wider, I nodded. *"Please."*

Wasting no more time, he leaned forward on the bed, nestling himself between my thighs, my body trembling with anticipation. It had been so long since I'd had a man who wanted to make me feel good, if I ever had. To be honest, I wasn't sure I'd ever been with a man who put my pleasure first.

"This may be a bad idea," he said, sending my heart into my stomach, worried he'd changed his mind.

Pulling myself up on my elbows, I looked down at his eyes, trying to decipher if he was joking, but all I found him doing was staring at my center. "Why would you say that?"

He licked his lips again and shook his head, taking a moment to answer. "Because after seeing how stunning you are like this, seeing how wet you are for me and tasting how sweet you are, it's going to be really fucking difficult to keep my cock in my pants."

Huffing, I laid back on the bed. "Well... I already said you don't have to, but I respect your boundaries like you respect mine."

Although I expected him to respond again—to pass a little more banter my way—he didn't. Instead, he kissed his way up my thigh, skipping over my pussy and then kissing down the other, teasing me. My hips rolled of their own accord—my pussy trying to get closer to his mouth when he kept moving away.

Just when I was about to beg him again, he leaned in, sliding his tongue all the way up my center from my entrance to my clit. The gasp that left my mouth with that first touch was near animalistic. I'd never felt anything so good, until he did it again.

And again.

And again.

My eyes rolled back into my head, and I could do nothing but tilt my head back and moan as he forced me to feel everything—his tongue dipping into my entrance, his lips against my clit, his breath in my pussy—so that, even when his mouth wasn't there, I could still feel him.

It was too much—*too good*. I rolled my hips more, begging for the orgasm that was brewing inside of me. As if he could read my mind, his tongue flicked against my swollen bundle of nerves, fast and hard, as he slid one finger, and then another inside me. With expert precision that I couldn't think about without getting jealous, he thrusted into me, rubbing against the sensitive spot inside as he worshiped me with his tongue.

It didn't take long for him to push me over that edge. Before I knew what hit me, I screamed, my nails digging into his skin as my orgasm made my entire body feel like it was on fire. Thighs shaking, I rode out the waves of pleasure, holding him in place as he continued playing my body like a fiddle. He didn't stop until every tremor settled, and I was limp against the sheets, sweating and sated.

I could feel his smirk on my pussy as he licked at the mess he'd made, and I was still gasping for breath when he pulled his fingers out of me and licked them clean. Their absence left me almost empty inside, like I needed more of him—*all* of him—but I knew it wouldn't happen, at least not yet. Although I wanted him more than anything, I was just relieved he was no longer rejecting me.

When my eyes flicked up to his, my cheeks still warm from my climax, his own were almost black with desire, his pupils blown wide and his body tense. "I could spend the rest of my life between your thighs," he rasped, pressing a kiss to my lips. "But we really should not go any further tonight. We need to take our time."

I knew it was the right thing to do, but I was having a harder and harder time caring what was right, especially when what was wrong felt so damn good.

Once Bane and I climbed out of bed, I took a shower while he watched the video. Although I'd told him I wanted to watch it also, I agreed to let him watch it first to make sure it was something I wanted to see. I didn't like the idea of being in the dark, but there wasn't much I could do with the information from the video anyway. At that moment, I was a passenger in my own life. Phantom and Bane were taking care of everything for me when it came to Joshua, and to my alleged disappearance, but I didn't mind. Out of everyone in my life, I trusted Bane the most.

When I finished showering, I returned to the living room. Already sitting on the sofa in front of his laptop, Bane's face was so lined in deep contemplation he didn't notice me walk in.

"Hey. How was the broadcast?"

Jolting at my voice, he twisted to look at me as I crossed the room, a smile tugging up the side of his lips. "How was your shower?"

When I passed beside him, he reached out, pulling me onto his lap and leaning in to kiss me on the cheek. "Let's put it this way, after the people of New Orleans see that, there will be many who'll be out for revenge against Joshua, and there will be very few who'll believe anything he says ever again."

CHAPTER 27

The Savior

I was in real trouble and I knew it, but I'd done it to myself. Never before had I been unable to control my desire for a woman. Before we returned inside the cabin, I had made my decision about me and Scarlett clear, but the moment she'd touched my face and told me to let her choose for herself—the moment she told me that I was what she wanted—I'd melted into her as though I had never said I wouldn't. I'd completely given in to the undeniable chemistry between us. There was no way either of us could predict how it would play out between us, but we both knew there was something there, so I'd agreed to give it a chance. From deciding against moving forward altogether, my face had ended up right between her thighs, the sweet taste of her still on my tongue. It had taken everything in me not to take things all the way, and all I hoped in the afterglow of making her come on my tongue was that I wouldn't hurt her.

With Scarlett curled up beside me on the sofa, several things swam through my mind—things that didn't revolve around burying myself in her pussy. The first was her father. I still hadn't told her that her father was involved in organized crime, and I didn't know how she would respond once I did. I didn't know if she would be furious with me for keeping it a secret from her. I hadn't known for a long time, but I should have told her as soon as I'd found out. The other issue plaguing me, as I rubbed my thumb across the palm of her hand, was the video and the fall out it would cause.

Swallowing back my hesitation, I leaned forward and turned my laptop back on. I had already watched the video while she was in the shower, and I wasn't looking forward to her seeing it. "So, should we get this over with and just watch it?"

Scarlett shrugged but still twisted to face the screen. "May as well. Then maybe we can enjoy the rest of our night."

Turning her gaze up to meet mine, her cheeks flushed, the sight stiffening my cock when I'd only jerked off fifteen minutes before. The minute she'd jumped into the shower, I'd had no choice but to hide in my bedroom and beat my meat like a horny teenager. It was pathetic but was the only thing that could possibly keep me from rutting her like an animal.

"I meant, watch a movie or play a game," she said, ramming her shoulder into mine, her cheeks burning redder. "You need to get your mind out of the gutter."

Chuckling, I clicked through the commands on the video player. She was a dirty little minx, and we both knew it. I was certainly not complaining. "You'll need to get yours out of the gutter first, because you're the naughty little girl who keeps pulling me in there."

With my finger on the play button, I leaned over and kissed her on the cheek. "Please let me know if you want me to turn it off and I will, okay? There's no shame in you not watching it."

With no other objections, I hit play, hoping the contents of the video wouldn't upset her more.

When the recording started, it was in the middle of the five o'clock local news broadcast, the male and female anchors sitting at their horseshoe-shaped desk as they dished out the top news of the day.

About five minutes into their scripted lines, the screen went all black, a message saying "Incoming breaking news" scrolling across the bottom of the screen like the warning of an approaching storm.

A few moments later, the solid black screen gave way to a nondescript room. The silhouette of a man sat in a chair in front of the camera, his entire face and body in deep shadows. I knew it was Phantom, but there would have been no way anyone else would be able to figure out who it was from what they could see.

Using software to change his voice, he started to speak. "Dear people of New Orleans, I have breaking news on the case of Scarlett Prejean, the missing wife of businessman and financier, Joshua Prejean. First, I have a recording I must play for you. This will not be suitable for children."

The moment Phantom stopped speaking, the recording began to play, the voices making Scarlett gasp.

Pausing the video, I turned to her. "Do you want me to turn it off? It's okay if you don't want to watch it."

She shook her head, but with her hands still covering her mouth, I wasn't convinced. "Is that the—"

"Is it the recording of when I met with Joshua? Yes."

"Won't people recognize your voice?"

I shook my head, pulling her closer. "No. Phantom used a software to change my voice, but Joshua's voice is crystal clear."

Once she nodded and melted against my side again, I pressed play to continue the video, knowing the worst was yet to come.

Scarlett and I watched the dark screen in silence as my recorded conversation with her husband played. With her remaining curled against my side, she did not cry as she listened to the heinous things Joshua wanted done to her. Her strength blew me away. In a way, she reminded me of my sister—in her strength—not in how badly I wanted to fuck her.

For a moment, I wondered if I would let the two of them meet one day, but I shoved the thought away quickly. I never let anyone get that close. I wasn't ruling out letting Scarlett in, but I just wasn't ready yet. Although I'd all but let her think I would let her be the one to decide if I was good enough for her, I didn't think I was ready for that yet either. However, since I seemed to be incapable of turning away from her as though she had cast some sort of spell on me, I guessed I was the one who didn't have a choice. If I were being honest, I didn't want to fight it anymore, but that didn't mean I was willing to sleep with her—at least not without my clothes on. She may have thought she was ready for us to have sex, but I knew better. The last thing I wanted was to destroy her, and I was still convinced that was what I would do. We'd already moved too far too quickly.

When the recording of my meeting with Joshua went silent, the focus fell back to Phantom's silhouette, still much too shaded to make out his features.

"If you listened to the recording I just played," he said, his voice still obscured by voice changing software. "Then you now understand that every claim Joshua Prejean has made was a lie. Well... everything except the claim that his bank accounts have been frozen. That is true, but they haven't been frozen for the reason he thinks they have. I will talk about that in a moment."

He shifted on his chair, the dark shading following his movements. "First, I wanted to assure Scarlett's family and friends she is very much alive, and she is safe. Let's just say that the hired assassin was a better man than her abusive husband ever was."

As the shadow of Phantom was replaced by a white screen, I couldn't help but chuckle at his comment. Scarlett may have agreed, but I had many victims who would have begged to differ.

Although we could no longer see Phantom on the screen, he once again began to speak, but this time, his words began scrolling up the screen like the credits of a movie.

"Joshua Prejean's accounts have been frozen, but not because his wife has stolen from him. It could be argued that much of his money is hers, and she will get her fair share, but Joshua Prejean's accounts have been hacked into and frozen because most of his money has been acquired by unethical and illegal means. I will leave you with a list of all the businesses and individuals he has screwed out of money, as well as all the entities who are in his pocket, or the other way around. The city of New Orleans and its citizens can decide what to do with the information."

The credits played for much longer than expected, since Phantom had found a laundry list of names that needed to go on it, but as the credits came to a halt, I turned to Scarlett, studying her face for any signs of distress. But instead, she just looked relieved. "Thank you," she whispered, her voice hoarse from all the crying she had done earlier that night, and probably a bit from our time in her bed. "Thank you for everything."

I gave her a small smile, pulling her closer. "You don't have to thank me. I did what I had to do to keep you safe and find you justice."

Nodding, she rested her head on my shoulder. "I know. But I'm grateful, nonetheless."

We sat there for a few moments, before I cleared my throat, dread tightening my windpipe as I thought about what I still needed to do. "Listen, Scarlett, I know you've been through a lot, and I don't want to add to that. But there's something I still have to tell you."

She looked up at me, her big brown eyes searching mine, the worry in them clear, and once again that night, it made me feel like shit. "What is it?"

Taking a deep breath, I tried to gather my thoughts, hating I was about to hurt her again. "It's about your father."

CHAPTER 28

The Survivor

S itting on the sofa with Bane, the air hung heavy around us, my breath lodged in my throat as I readied myself for his next words. But before he could say them, the sound of boards creaking echoed through the silent night. Bane's eyes flicked to the side, his body language tightening. The doorknob jiggled once ... twice ... and then he reached for my arm, pulling me into the bedroom.

Seconds passed as we scrambled to shove essential items into packs and pull on heavy boots and coats. There was no time to speak, or even to think, as sounds of someone trying to break into the cottage drove my heartbeat to the speed of a racehorse. He strapped weapons onto his belt and grabbed his laptop just before he slid open a hidden panel in the back of his closet and pushed me inside, closing it behind us.

The dim light of a cell phone flashlight lit our way as he led me down a narrow staircase into the hidden basement below the cottage, the footsteps above us telling me that whoever had been trying to get into the cottage had finally succeeded. I didn't dare ask Bane who he thought it was, not with the risk of my voice alerting them of our presence.

He dragged me toward the back door, his hand warm and calloused around mine. "We have to go. *Now*."

Although my heart pounded in my chest, the familiar rush of panic and adrenaline coursing through my veins, I didn't dare argue. A moment later, we plunged into the forest, navigating between gnarled branches that clawed at my clothes and made walking difficult.

Guiding us forward, his gaze scanned the terrain for any signs of danger, but we didn't see or hear anyone. A black SUV had blocked the entrance of the driveway, but whoever had come to the cottage all seemed to be inside. Still, the hair on the back of my neck stood on end as though I was being watched.

With my boots stumbling over twisted roots and underbrush, I struggled to keep up with his brisk pace.

"Stay close," he said, not slowing his steps.

I gritted my teeth as his hand tightened around mine, determination setting in. I refused to be the reason we were caught.

The forest thickened around us as we moved through trees and bushes. My lungs burned as I gasped for air, sweat dripping down my neck. Still, he showed no signs of stopping. His resolve was iron; his focus unwavering. I squeezed his hand, not daring to speak. We had to keep going. Together, I had to believe we could make it through anything.

I wasn't sure how far we'd traveled when the sound of twigs snapping somewhere behind us made my heart leap into my throat. Bane's grip tightened on my hand and we picked up our pace, ducking under low-hanging branches. Voices drifted through the forest, growing louder with each step.

Panic threatened to overtake me, my chest tightening until I could barely breathe, knowing they were gaining on us. It was only a matter of minutes before they spotted us, before—

"There!" A shout rang out behind us as a gunshot split the air. The bullet whizzed past my head, biting into the tree beside me. I screamed, nearly tripping over my own feet.

Bane yanked me forward, breaking into a run as more gunshots followed. "Don't stop!" Pulling me off the winding path, we forged ahead into denser brush. The terrain grew treacherous, sloping downward before dropping off into a rocky ravine.

I scrambled to keep my footing, heart pounding wildly against my ribs. As we slid down the ravine, a narrow stone path came into view along one side. Bane dragged me onto the path without slowing, his chest heaving.

The sound of rushing water filled my ears. Up ahead, the path ended at a cliff overlooking the churning river.

Skidding to a stop, his eyes scanned the cliff and river below. I peered over the edge, a gasp escaping my lips, terror numbing my limbs. The drop was at least fifty feet, ending in a maelstrom of whitewater rapids and jagged boulders, the moon highlighting the danger below.

There was nowhere left to run. We were trapped.

Bane's gaze flickered to mine, his chest rising and falling at a rapid pace. The shouts behind us were growing louder, nearly upon us. I could see the panic brewing in his eyes as his hands tightened around my arms.

"We have to jump."

Although I expected the words, they still chilled my blood when he spoke them. I stared at him like he was insane. "What? No!"

"It's our only chance!" His eyes pleaded with me as another gunshot rang out. "I don't know who they are, Scarlett, but it's real fucking possible they'll kill us if we don't. The current is strong—it'll carry us away from them. Please, Little Red, trust me!"

My heart slammed against my ribs, torn between the churning river below and the gunmen behind, but I knew he was right. It was either a risky plunge or facing certain death.

Gritting my teeth, I nodded, and he pulled me into his arms without another word, his embrace iron clad. I gripped him as though he was all I had left in the world, our chests pressing together as we backed toward the edge of the cliff.

The river stretched endlessly before us, roaring and unforgiving. Bane's warmth was my only solace against the icy grip of fear threatening to consume me. Breathing him in, I summoned every ounce of courage I had left.

"Together," he said, his breath hot against my ear. I nodded into his chest, squeezing my eyes shut.

The gunmen emerged behind us, their shouts piercing the air. Bane's grip on me tightened impossibly, and then—

We were falling.

The cliff crumbled away beneath us as we plunged into the open air, tumbling toward the rapids below. A scream tore from my throat, lost to the wind whipping around us. The river rushed up to meet us, cold and unyielding, as we crashed into its depths.

In a blink, the current seized me, tossing me around like a rag doll beneath its surface. I struggled for purchase, kicking against the tug of the rapids. Breaking through to the surface, I gasped for air, fingers clawing at the water.

"Bane!"

In the darkness, I scanned the churning river. Debris and froth obscured my vision, a maze of obstacles standing between us.

He was gone—swallowed whole by the water in a matter of seconds. Panic swelled in my heart, stealing the breath from my lungs. I couldn't lose him. Not now, not after everything.

"Bane!" I screamed again, fighting against the current dragging me under once more.

Kicking with all my might, I propelled myself forward, dodging trees and rocks jutting from the riverbed.

A dark shape flashed in my peripheral vision, and I swung toward it with renewed hope. Bane emerged from the whitewash, his face contorted in a mask of determination. Our eyes met across the river, understanding passing between us in an instant.

The current, however, had other plans. Before I could push off toward him, it seized me again, hurtling me in the opposite direction. I reached for him, desperation crushing my chest as I watched the distance between us grow. The river had won.

Darkness loomed at the edges of my vision, exhaustion and panic threatening to overtake me. As my limbs began to fail, a single thought echoed in my mind, refusing to fade. I *had* to find Bane. Against all odds, I had to find him.

Through sheer force of will, I fought my way back to the surface, dragging in ragged breaths. The river stretched like a black void before me, but I would not give up. Not until he was safe in my arms once more. The current could not have him.

I would not let it.

The branch I clung to was my only lifeline in a sea of water that threatened to swallow me whole. My fingers were numb from the icy chill seeping into my bones, but I held on for dear life. Although it felt like I had been there for hours, I knew it couldn't have been more than a few minutes. My strength was fading fast, my arms trembling from the effort to keep my head above the surface.

"Bane!"

Scanning the surface of the water, my throat was raw from screaming, the hope that he would appear only crushing me when no one came. I was alone.

A sob welled in my chest as I struggled to keep my grip on the branch. I wasn't sure how much longer I could hold on—how much longer I could fight.

My fingers started to slip. I squeezed my eyes shut, steeling myself for the icy grip of the water to claim me once more.

Just when I was about to let go, I heard it—a shout in the distance, barely audible above the river's roar.

"Scarlett!"

My eyes flew open as a dark figure emerged from the rapids, fighting his way toward me against the current, sending my heart soaring in my chest. Bane grabbed my arm just as my fingers lost their grip on the branch, pulling me close against him. "I've got you. You're safe, Little Red. I've got you."

The sob broke free and I wrapped my arms around him, clinging to him as fiercely as I had clung to that branch. He held me close, struggling to stay afloat as the icy water buffeted our exhausted bodies, but I knew he wouldn't let me go.

Angling us toward the riverbank, he kicked with all his might against the current.

At last, his feet hit solid ground, and he dragged us onto the riverbank, collapsing beside me on the rocky shore.

For a long moment we just lay there, panting and shivering, staring up at the night sky. I wasn't sure where our pursuers were, but I was freezing, and didn't know if I would ever be warm again. The forest loomed dark and dense around us, shadows dancing in the dim moonlight that filtered through the treetops. Only a few feet away from us, the river rushed onward, a constant reminder of the danger we had narrowly escaped.

When I turned to look at Bane, he was already watching me, his light eyes nearly clear in the moonlight.

"You came back for me."

Reaching toward me, he stroked my cheek. "I will always come for you."

A tear slid down my cheek, all my insecurities flooding to the surface. "Promise?"

He brought our joined hands to his lips, kissing my knuckles. "I promise. You're mine now, Little Red, and I protect what's mine."

For a moment, all I could do was stare at him, surprised at his response, but that wore off quickly and then I surged forward and kissed him. He didn't hesitate, wrapping his arms around me and pulling me on top of him.

When at last we broke apart, breathless, he cupped the back of my head, pulling my forehead to rest against his. "I'm still not good enough for you, though."

Unable to help myself, I laughed. "You just saved my life. *Again.* I think that earns you a few points." A cool breeze whipped past us, causing my teeth to chatter. "It-it's freezing out here."

Bane pressed a kiss to my damp and tangled hair. "I know. Just let me hold you for another minute." Wrapping his arms tighter around my body, he rolled us until I was below him, pressing another kiss to my lips. "I thought I'd lost you. When I couldn't find you in the water, I—" His voice broke, his eyes squeezing shut.

Shifting in his arms, I reached up to cup his cheek. "But you found me ... so, thank you."

He leaned into my touch, covering my hand with his before pulling himself onto his knees. "We have to keep moving before they pick up our trail again. And we need to find a way to get dry."

CHAPTER 29

The Survivor

Leaving the churning river behind us, Bane and I pushed through the dense underbrush, thorns and branches tearing at our clothes and skin. The forest seemed never-ending. The trees were clustered so tightly together it was difficult to see more than a few feet ahead. He led the way, using a large hunting knife to hack away vines and clear a path. I followed closely behind, stumbling over roots and rocks, my legs burning with exertion. The farther we went, the darker and more ominous the forest became, but at least there were no bullets flying past us. Shadows deepened between the trees, playing tricks on my exhausted mind. I flinched at every snapped twig or rustling bush, imagining lurking dangers that probably weren't there.

Pausing, Bane turned to face me, his eyes filled with concern. "Are you doing okay?"

Although I was barely holding it together, I nodded. I refused to be the weak link—the one who slowed us down.

248

He studied me a moment before dipping his head. "There are some cabins not far from here ... a campground. I'm sure one of them is empty that we can break into so we can rest in for a while."

Just the thought of stopping was bliss. Relief washed over me, my legs wobbling with the promise of respite.

Wasting no more time, we continued on with renewed urgency. The promise of somewhere to hide from our pursuers, if only briefly, gave us the energy to push forward through the hellish terrain. Finally, the campground came into view, the small wooden structures scattered throughout the forest for people to rent. *Sanctuary.*

With it still being the off-season, there was more than one empty cabin, so he was able to pick the lock in the outermost building, allowing us inside. The moment the door opened, I collapsed onto the floor, every muscle in my body screaming. We were both filthy, exhausted wrecks, but we had survived the river, and at that moment, we were still free.

Closing the door, he stacked logs in the fireplace, lighting the fire before he slumped down beside me, dropping his head into his hands. I could see his powerful shoulders rising and falling as he caught his breath.

"You think we lost them?"

He lifted his head, his piercing eyes meeting mine. "For now, but we can't stay long. We should dry off in front of the fire while we can. I don't want you getting hypothermia."

With a gentle squeeze to my thigh, he stood and pulled off his shirt, hanging it on the rack in front of the fireplace. I followed suit, not caring that he saw me in my bra. After having his face between my thighs, we were past that point. As much as I needed rest, the urgency of our situation left no time for indulgence. "What's the plan?"

His jaw tightened. "We keep moving. Head north through the mountains. With some luck, we can make it to the highway and find a car."

Setting his jeans aside, he closed the distance between us, moving a strand of wet hair from my face. "Hey. We're gonna make it through this. I promise." His voice was firm, but his eyes were soft. And despite everything, I believed him. If anyone could get us out of this, it was Bane.

"Here, sit down before you fall down." Wrapping a quilt around my shoulders, he guided me onto the sofa in front of the fire. I sank down beside him, too numb to resist. We were both down to our wet underwear, his black boxer briefs doing little to hide his assets in the firelight, and I couldn't help the heat that swirled low in my belly.

"I need to contact Phantom. My phone may have survived the river with its protective case, but my laptop wouldn't have. If I have a signal, then maybe he can get us out of here."

"First, let me see where you're hurt," he said, sliding off the sofa and kneeling before me, his large hands delicate as they examined the small gash on my arm. I winced as he cleaned away the blood and then wrapped it with a scrap of a clean dishrag he found in the kitchen. His touch was comforting, despite the sting. Craving the reassurance of another human being–of him—I found myself leaning into it.

His eyes met mine, his gaze intent. In the dim light of the cabin, his face seemed to soften. Neither of us spoke, the air heavy between us. Without a word, he wrapped his arms around me, pulling me against his body and pressing his lips to mine.

For a moment, everything else melted away. The danger. The fear. All that mattered was that moment—the warmth of his lips, the heat of him against me, and the softness of his tongue as it explored my mouth. The kiss was gentle at first, a soft exploration of one another that soon turned into something more.

As if they had been longing to touch me all along, his hands were everywhere at once. His lips caressed mine with every breath I took, his hands roamed down my back and pulled me closer until there was no space between us left to fill. He groaned as he deepened our kiss, a low rumble that vibrated through us both.

The heat of the fire licked at us as we clung to each other in the warmth and safety of the cabin, our bodies alive with a desperate hunger, exploring and tasting until I thought my heart would burst from my chest. His arms were strong around me, the urgency between us was undeniable, both of us wanting more despite knowing the moment could not last forever. But that moment was ours alone, just him and I, in the midst of a perilous journey taking what solace we could find in each other's embrace before having to return to the world outside the cabin. And because of that, every moment until then was one to be treasured.

CHAPTER 30

The Savior

Pulling Scarlett into my arms, I lifted her, claiming her lips as I carried her to the bed, all my previous hesitations burning away. I'd thought I'd lost her in that river. Experiencing something like that was enough to scare anyone's priorities into place.

The warmth from the fire reached us in the one room cabin, the dancing flames the only light as I laid her beautiful body down on the bed in front of me.

For a moment, all I could do was look at how stunning she was, running my fingertips over her curves, the swell of her breasts, and the flat plane of her stomach. Her lips were red and swollen from our kisses and her nipples hard from arousal. I wanted to touch every part of her, but I knew our time was limited.

"You are so damn perfect," I whispered.

"Bane..." Her voice was a breathless whisper, her dark eyes hungry for more.

Without another word, I lowered my face to hers, kissing her again. Her fingers tangled in my hair, a gentle tugging that only made me want her more.

I moved down her body, planting soft kisses down her neck, her shoulders, and the swell of her breastbone. All I wanted was to taste her again and have her writhing beneath me. Her strength was incredible. She'd kept up with me, clawing her way to freedom from the river. There was no way I would let anyone harm her again, not if I was still breathing. I would take care of her and show her what it truly meant to be loved and cherished.

I knew I could never have enough of her. After fighting it every day since I'd first laid eyes on her, the desire to lose myself in her was too much to bear.

Sliding her wet bra strap off her shoulder, I pressed my lips to her rounded breast, her sharp gasp of pleasure like a bolt of lightning striking through me. She trembled in my arms as my tongue found her skin, her hips arching up as I traced circles around her nipple. My fingers slid down the side of her ribcage, pulling her panties down over her hips. My fingertips trailed down her thigh, her eyes fluttering open when I slid them between her legs.

"Bane... *Please*..." The word held a thousand meanings, all of them more than I could bear to resist.

Scarlett's lips parted in a moan, her back arching as I kissed the tender skin on her stomach, her body trembling with anticipation. With her fingers in my hair, she guided me, spreading her legs as I kissed my way down her thigh.

When her legs parted, the sight of her center made my mouth water. I needed to taste her, to feel her skin against my tongue again.

She opened her legs wider, baring her perfect cunt to me, and I didn't hesitate to slide my tongue through her folds, pulling a gasp from deep in her chest. Her sounds were like music to my ears, the scent of her washing over me like a drug. Gripping my hair, her hips bucking up to me for more, as I sucked her clit between my teeth. I slid a finger inside of her, followed by another, her breath catching as I gave her what she needed.

"Oh, gods..." Her voice shook as I worked her clit and hit her G-spot with my fingers in thorough strokes.

Lifting my eyes, I admired her writhing body, my cock hard as stone against the mattress and needing her more than I needed the blood in my veins. Her eyes were half-open, her breath coming faster as I slid my fingers in and out of her, the sound of her wetness only making me want her more. I wanted to lose myself in her—to lose myself in the way she moaned—to lose myself in her body and never let go.

All of this was more, so much more, than I'd ever had... and with her, it was only the beginning.

"Bane ... I'm so close." Following her direction, I doubled my efforts, savoring how her moans got louder, how her walls tightened around my fingers.

"Oh, gods. Oh, gods. Oh, gods." Her back arched when she came, her body shaking as her thighs tightened around my head. Slowing my movements, I worked my tongue in soft circles until she calmed, pulling my fingers out of her and licking them clean.

"Oh... my gods." An expression of dazed pleasure colored her face when she looked down at me, her fingers running through my hair and urging me closer.

The fire crackled in the corner, its flames bathing us with warmth. Moving back up on the bed, I rested my body against hers, leaning in to kiss her as she wrapped her arm around my neck.

"Bane..." She breathed my name, her voice like a song between us.

I kissed her again, her breathing still heavy from her climax, her heart pounding in tandem with mine against my chest.

"Scarlett, we don't have to—" Although My cock was already straining against my boxer briefs, the thin fabric doing little to contain the erection it was struggling to hold back, the last thing I wanted was for her to feel forced to do anything she wasn't ready for. She'd done enough of that in her life. But before I finished my statement, her finger pressed against my lips.

"Don't try to give me an out, Bane. I don't want one. I need you." She looked at me, her face flushed, her dark eyes pleading with me.

"If we do this, Little Red, I want you to call me Ethan. I want you to know my real name." Although I expected her to recoil at the admission that I'd kept my real name from her, she didn't even flinch. It was like she already knew.

Reaching forward, she trailed her fingers down my cheek, the touch sending shivers all the way into my soul. "I want you, Ethan. I want you for who you are." Her voice was a whisper, the sound of her need echoing through me. Her eyes were dark, her body curled up against mine, the smooth curves of her begging for me to take her.

With the taste of her still on my tongue, I kissed her again, stoking a flame inside of me. "I'm already yours."

Wrapping her leg over my hip, her hand trailing down my chest, her soft fingers working their way between my legs, stroking my cock through my boxer briefs. Her eyes were on me, peeling back every layer and wall. "Then I need to feel you."

Unable to wait any longer, I slid my underwear down my hips and tossed them to the floor, my hard length standing at attention. Her eyes darted up to meet mine as her hand closed around it, stroking up and down in languid strokes. My cock responded instinctively, her every touch like an electric current beneath my skin. I hungered for her, my body desperate for hers like I would die without it.

Cheeks flushing a delicious shade of pink, she smiled at me as she laid back on the bed, spreading her legs in a silent invitation. Her folds glistened from how ready she was for me. I crawled over her, my cock desperate to be inside her.

Leaning in, I kissed her, my tongue exploring the depths of her mouth while my hand reached down and guided myself to her entrance, sliding my cock in her juices before I pushed myself inside. We both gasped as her body opened up to me, our eyes meeting when we realized we should have been touching each other all along. Our bodies melted together, moving in perfect harmony as we found our rhythm.

Her fingers clawed into my back and her legs wrapped tightly around me to pull me deeper but even after loosening her with my fingers, she was too tight to just let go. My cock throbbed with need, each stroke sending a white-hot jolt of pleasure through my veins. Her whimpers of pleasure only spurred me on. She was so wet, the sound of our bodies coming together echoing in the darkness.

Groaning at how good it felt, I pulled back and then thrust into her again, burying myself to the hilt. With her arms wrapped around me and her hands holding me close, her body undulated against mine, the passion of the moment intense enough to bring tears to my eyes.

Pleasure flooding her face, she threw her head back as she came, her raven hair spilling over the pillow. Her walls tightened around me forcing me to thrust in harder, her body pulling me deeper inside of her as her hips rocked against mine in a steady rhythm. Her spine stiffened and she arched her back up off the bed, her voice hoarse as she cried out.

My muscles tightened like I was about to burst. I kissed her, her tongue dancing with mine as I thrust into her, my eyes rolling back with how perfect she felt.

Although I wanted to make it last all night, it was too fucking good, so I was seconds away from exploding when I heard her soft whisper. "Come inside me."

Her words sent me over the edge, groaning into her neck as I did exactly what she demanded without a second thought. If she got pregnant, I would only worship her more. As I released inside her welcoming body, it was a torrent of sensation that robbed me of my breath.

When the tremors stopped, I collapsed on top of her, my arms on either side of her shoulders. Her eyes sparkled as she looked up at me, her beauty taking my breath away.

The moment was so perfect I didn't want to ruin it by speaking, so instead I chose to lie there with her in the firelight. As the blaze crackled in the background, Scarlett and my limbs intertwined. With me still inside of her, not wanting to leave her warmth, our bodies moved to the rhythm of the flames. I kissed her shoulder, her neck, her lips, savoring the taste of her as I pulled her closer... and closer.

When I finally stopped thrusting inside her, sated and exhausted, her breathing was slow and steady as she lay on her side, looking up at me with a smile on her face that told me she felt the same way.

Smiling back, I looked into her eyes, my heart pounding as I saw a wisp of fear still floating in their depths.

"Everything's going to be okay," I said, brushing a stray hair off her forehead and kissing her on the lips. I wanted to say more, but I didn't know how. All I knew for sure was that I couldn't get enough of her. She was mine.

Closing her eyes, she nodded, her body rising and falling with every breath as she drifted off to sleep. My eyes moved over her while she slept, barely able to believe that she was there with me.

"I love you," I whispered, surprised when the words left my mouth as easily as if I was taking a breath. Although I'd never said them to any woman aside from my sister and mother, I knew deep down in my heart that they were true.

As I closed my eyes, I listened to the sound of her breathing, wrapping my arm around her and pulling her closer. All I could think was that I never wanted to let her go, and I hoped I would never have to.

CHAPTER 31

The Survivor

*F*ootsteps, the crunch of leaves under heavy boots, woke me from a deep sleep. My heart seized, pulling me up from my safe place in the bed where Bane and I had made love.

In an instant, he was on his feet, his body coiled tight as a spring. His eyes met mine, his finger signaling toward our clothes and his weapons as the other lifted to his mouth.

I nodded as he moved, slipping to the floor between the bed and the wall, my pulse pounding in my ears, not understanding how they'd tracked us to the cabin so quickly. But unless it was someone checking into the cabin in the middle of the night, or a very curious bear, it was our pursuers.

A moment later, he slid my clothes to me, pulling on his own as he positioned himself between me and the entrance.

The footsteps halted just outside the cabin door. If there had been any question it could have just been a camper, coming to check into the cabin for a getaway, that thought was dashed the second we heard the click of a gun cocking. Bane's jaw clenched, his muscles taut.

Heart dropping into my stomach, I sucked in a breath, watching him quietly. There was so much I wanted to say. I wanted to beg him not to sacrifice himself for my sake, because I knew that was exactly what he intended to do, but before I could speak, the door burst open, and all hell broke loose.

Bane moved with calculated precision as the five armed men flooded into the cabin. His fist smashed into the first man's nose in a spray of blood, bones crunching from the impact. Before the man knew what was happening, Bane grabbed the man's gun, turning it on the others who were just realizing their ambush had failed.

Gunshots split the air as he opened fire, dropping two more men in quick succession. The remaining men scattered for cover, returning fire. Using the furniture as a shield, Bane fired back, holding his own against multiple adversaries.

Unable to tear my eyes away, I huddled behind the bed, hands pressed over my ears. I had never seen anything like it. He was death incarnate, an unstoppable force of vengeance cutting down anyone who stood in his path, but the men kept coming, wave after wave. No matter how many he gunned down, more appeared to take their place. It was clear they were wearing him down. I could see exhaustion creeping into the corded muscles of his back, his breath coming harder. He wouldn't last much longer at the pace it was going, and it terrified me. For the life of me, I didn't understand what they wanted. There was no reason for my husband to put so much effort into finding me. It just didn't make any sense.

As Bane moved to refill his magazine, a shot caught him in the shoulder, making him stagger. Biting back a scream, my fingers dug into the floorboards. His eyes found mine through the chaos, full of fury and regret. I knew then what that look meant. It was a fight he couldn't win, but he would die on his feet before he let them take me.

Tears blurred my vision. I wanted to run to him—to fight at his side—but I was frozen where I crouched. I was powerless as the men closed in for the kill.

The circle of enemies tightened around the man I loved, their guns leveled at his head. His muscles trembled with exhaustion, soaked in blood and sweat, but his icy eyes burned with defiance. He would not make this easy for them.

With a guttural roar, he surged forward, his knife finding throats and stomachs. The gunshots were deafening in the small cabin, and I couldn't tell if the screams were his or theirs.

Then, when he rose to his feet to run to me, a blow to the back of his head sent him crashing to his knees. I cried out as the group of men swarmed him, raining down blows until he lay crumpled and unmoving in a heap on the floor.

"No! Bane!" I screamed, but rough hands seized my arms, dragging me from my hiding place. Straining against the iron grips holding me back, I fought with nails and teeth, but it was useless. They shoved me toward the door, heedless of my screams.

"Bane!" My heart splintered in my chest as I tried to throw myself on Bane's body. I was desperate to end his suffering, but they yanked me to my feet and held me back, kicking and screaming. His eyes flickered open, dazed with pain, focusing on my face. I saw his lips shape my name, his hand reaching for me, but no sound came out before they forced me from the cabin and into the cold rain. The last glimpse I caught of my savior was his body lying broken amidst the carnage, my heart shattering with it, but I swore to myself if I made it out of this alive, I would find my way back to him. No matter what it took. In the short time I'd known him, he'd become everything to me. There was no way I could just walk away from him—pretend like none of it had ever happened—even if I did get out of it somehow.

I stumbled through the dark woods, prodded along by the barrel of a gun. Rain poured down in sheets, plastering my hair to my face and mingling with the tears on my cheeks. Sobs wracked my body, as much from fear as grief. I didn't know if Bane was alive or dead. The *not knowing* was a knife twisting in my gut.

When we came upon a clearing where several SUVs idled, headlights cutting through the gloom, an older man in a suit with dark sunglasses stood waiting, an oily smile spreading across his face at the sight of me. I didn't know who he was, but anyone wearing dark sunglasses on a rainy night was a psycho.

"Well done, boys," he said, as they shoved me to my knees in the mud before him. "You've brought me quite the prize."

"Who are you?" Twisting in their grip, I lifted my chin, glaring daggers up at him through my sodden hair. "What do you want from me?"

He crouched down, grasping my chin with his ringed fingers. "You, my dear, are worth a lot to some very important people." He shrugged, lifting my chin more. "You are a very nice bargaining chip to have in my pocket."

My heart pounding hard enough for him to hear it, I wrenched my head from his grasp. I had to get away somehow. For Bane. For Ethan.

"Bargaining chip for what?" My question fell on deaf ears as the man running the show straightened, all pretense of civility gone.

"Take her back to headquarters," he barked, sauntering toward one of the vehicles.

As they dragged me to my feet, he added, "And if she causes trouble, don't hesitate to punish her."

Bile rising into my throat, I swallowed hard, my mind racing. There was no way I would go without a fight, but I had no weapons.

"Let go of me!"

Balling my hands into fists, I tried to fight my way free, but they were too strong. Dragging me to the SUV, the two men forced me inside one of the vehicles and kicked the door closed, tires spinning in the mud as we sped away from the clearing. The separation from Bane was like tearing out my heart, the physical pain more crippling the farther we drove away from the forest. His strength was like a living thing, pulsing in my blood and bones, lending me his power. I strained against the seatbelt, but they were too well-armed to fight them with my bare hands.

Bane would come for me. I could feel it in my soul—and when he did—we would make them pay for what they'd done. I steeled my resolve, knowing I would survive, and when I did, I would find my way to him, and together, we would show them what it meant to test the strength of our bond.

CHAPTER 32

The Savior

I awoke with a start, my head throbbing, unsure how long I'd been out. The dim light of the moon filtering through the broken windows did little to illuminate the destroyed cabin, but I could see blood and bullet holes covering nearly every surface in the light it provided. Blinking, I tried to clear the fog from my mind. It took me a moment to realize what had happened, but then it all came flooding back—the ambush, the fight, and Scarlett's scream as they dragged her away. *Scarlett*! My heart seized with panic and I bolted upright, ignoring the pain and wave of dizziness that washed over me.

Nothing mattered but finding her. I couldn't let anything happen to her, not after everything we'd been through together. I loved her. There was no doubt, as scary as that was.

The creaking floorboards protested as I hauled myself to my feet. Blood dripped from my busted lip, leaving a coppery tang in my mouth. I didn't have time to tend to my own injuries—Scarlett needed me. The bullet wound in my shoulder throbbed, but it had been a clean shot, so I didn't have to dig the bullet out. A small mercy. Still, it would need bandages and antibiotics. Both of which I had at my cottage. I wrapped my shirt around the wound as I walked around the room and gathered my things.

Wasting not a second longer, I slipped a knife into my boot and tucked my gun into the back of my jeans. Fire surged through my veins with my need to get to Scarlett, but I had to be smart about my next moves, which wouldn't be easy since I had no idea who'd even attacked us. Rushing in without a plan would only get us both killed, but every minute I delayed was another minute she spent in their clutches.

No matter who they were, the cabin wouldn't provide any answers. I needed to get back to the city, see what my contacts knew about the Mob's movements. With any luck, I could pick up my Little Red's trail before they got too far.

I *couldn't* fail her.

Gripping my bag, I strode out the door and into the shadowed forest, leaving the cabin in flames behind me. If I had to burn the entire world down, I would find her, and gods help anyone who stood in my way.

After searching the immediate area for tire tracks or any trace of her and finding none, I headed in the direction of my cottage. With fractured ribs and untold other injuries, it was not an easy trek as I moved through the forest on silent feet, senses on high alert. The trees were dense there, branches clawing at my skin as I slipped between their gnarled trunks. It would have been easy for someone to hide amongst the shadows, waiting to ambush me, so I couldn't let my guard down, not even for a second. Letting my guard down in the cabin the night before had gotten us attacked—*it had gotten her taken.*

With worry and anger warring within me, I clenched my teeth until my jaw hurt and picked up my pace to a near jog, the gloomy forest matching my mood. I should never have let my guard down and given into my desires. I'd failed her, and now she was paying the price.

Although my phone had survived the river, I didn't chance using it as I traversed the forest, not that I would have had the signal to do so. With the Mob finding us in the middle of nowhere, I couldn't take the chance that they'd somehow cracked into that device. I had other burners at the cottage, so I intended to contact Phantom once I had a new one. I'd worked with Phantom long enough to know he wouldn't double cross me, but it was possible that whoever had found us had their own team of skilled hackers who'd beaten us at our own game. The thought pissed me off.

As I walked, my fingers brushed over the hilt of my knife, taking comfort in its solid presence. The assholes who took Scarlett had no idea who they were dealing with. I hadn't built my reputation as one of the most dangerous men in the city by being careless or squeamish. People may have not known my name, but they knew my work, and I couldn't wait to teach each one of them a very valuable lesson for stealing my girl.

The trees began to thin as I got closer to my cottage, so I slowed my pace to make sure none of the intruders had lingered. If I was lucky, they'd taken for granted that I was dead, that they no longer had to worry about me coming for her, and I would catch them when they were least expecting it. Then, when I finally found the men who had taken her, I would show no mercy. They would regret the day they ever crossed me. I would make sure of it.

Crouching in the bushes, I watched my cottage for several moments, making sure no one had stayed behind on my property.

When I was sure the coast was clear, I left the cover of the forest and darted across the yard, sliding into the basement entrance. As soon as I was inside my cottage, I moved in the shadows, making sure it was empty before going into my bedroom.

Opening the hidden compartment in my closet, I opened the safe and pulled out a backup burner phone, weapons, and an extra laptop, filling my bags with everything I needed. With the worst of my wounds cleaned and bandaged, and the first aid kit in my hand, I headed back outside, setting the security system before securing the door.

I scanned the area as I ran to the barn on the back of the property. Even with the pain stabbing and throbbing in every part of my body, I wasted no time climbing into my car and leaving the Alabama mountains in the rearview mirror, heading back toward New Orleans. The pain would only serve as more fuel to find her and kill them.

With six hours of road still in front of me in the dead of the night, I pulled out the burner phone on the seat beside me and dialed Phantom's number, his voice coming through on the first ring. "Hey Boss, I've been waitin' to hear from ya. Everything okay?"

I clenched my jaw. There was no time for pretenses. "Scarlett's been taken. I think it was Ivy's gang, but it could be a rival. I need everything you can dig up on them. Location, members, plans. And I needed it yesterday."

Phantom whistled low through the phone. "Can't say I'm surprised after the broadcast last night, but I'm shocked they found you." Keys clacked rapidly on his end. "I'm on it, Boss. I'll tap into the traffic cams around where she was taken, see if I can track where they went." For a moment, Phantom went silent, but when he came back, his voice was hesitant. "You planning on going in after them by yourself?"

For as long as Phantom had been taking my calls, he already knew the answer to that question. "Aside from you, I work alone."

Phantom chuckled. "Somehow I knew you'd say that. Alright, gimme a few hours to work my magic here. I'll call you when I get something."

I tossed it back onto the seat, burying the gas pedal below my boot. Given the silence, Scarlett's absence pressed down on me like an enveloping dark cloud. I tightened my grip on the steering wheel. Every mile that brought me closer to the city also brought me closer to the danger she faced, and the thought of her in danger burned the back of my throat with dread. My thoughts spun as I drove. As the winding roads of the north Alabama mountains gave way to the flat expanse of Louisiana, all I pictured was my Little Red in danger. This was a race against time, and I could not afford to make any mistakes, nor could I afford to lose my head.

When I finally parked my car in the garage at my building in New Orleans, the familiar sights and sounds of the city did not help to ease my anxiety. Unlike the fresh, cool air of the mountains, the air in the city was thick with humidity. The heat was oppressive even in mid-October.

The smell of donuts wafted through the open windows from the bakery around the block, making my stomach grumble, but I ignored it. My safe haven, normally a place of solace, now felt like a temporary stop on my mission to rescue Scarlett, and I didn't have time to get comfortable. I *would not* take comfort until I had her back with me.

Unlocking my door, I scanned the area around my entrance, holding my breath as I placed my ear against the door. I'd made the decision to return to my own apartment at that moment, but I knew it would only be temporary until I found Scarlett. When I had her back, the Mob would know I was alive, so I would have to take her to a safe house elsewhere. Although I was not sure if they knew my true identity, I couldn't take any chances with her life. But when it was just me, I dared them to find me at home. If they did, it would only make it easier for me to find their hideout, and that's where I would find my Little Red.

Taking a deep breath, I stepped into my apartment, shutting and locking the door behind me. I was unable to sit still and unable to sleep, so I ate, drank, and then immediately began to gather the tools I would need to face the men who took her. My living room table was laden with guns, ammunition, and a bulletproof vest, but as I prepared for battle, my thoughts continued to plague me. I was haunted by her warm smile and gentle touch, reminding me of what lay ahead and what was at stake.

Shaking my head, I tried to clear my thoughts, needing to focus, but it was useless. In life, I was a patient man, but not at that moment. At that moment, knowing my girl was somewhere afraid and alone, I could have breathed fire.

I glanced at my phone, which was still silent, as I yanked my shirt off and tossed it to the ground, wincing as my injuries ached. Although I wanted to feel the pain—I deserved the pain—I knew I couldn't continue to fight if I wasn't at my best. So, although I deserved to suffer, I went into my bathroom and took a shower, cleaning the blood and grime from my body, watching the crimson water swirl down the drain. When I was out, I cleaned and bandaged my wounds before returning to my office. My shoulder hurt like hell, but I took medication that wouldn't dull my senses, and let the pain that remained fuel the fight that was ahead.

In the hours since I had given Phantom his orders, I had not spoken with him. The only updates he had sent me were through messages, and they had not been enough to tell me where to begin. Without more information, I was dead in the water.

As I sat down in front of my computer, I booted up the secure communication software on the device. The screen flickered to life, casting a soft blue glow over the dimly lit room. My fingers pounded across the keyboard, inputting the necessary codes and passwords I needed as I placed the earbud in my ear and called him.

"Hey, Boss. I'm still cracking away at this," Phantom said, his voice crackled through the speakers. Despite the slight distortion from our secure line, I could still make out the familiar sound of him munching on his favorite snack—popcorn, probably cheesy. "But I'm working on back doors into a few things."

"First, we need to locate her. Have you hacked into the roadside cameras and security cameras along the route to see if there's any footage of her being taken?"

"Already on it," Phantom replied, the tapping of his keys echoing through the line. "In the meantime, we should strategize on a plan to get her back."

My mind raced as I considered the best strategy when I had no idea what I was up against. Just realizing how out-manned I was had me gripping the edge of the table until my knuckles turned white. "If they know I'm still alive—which I'm hoping they don't—they'll be expecting us to come at them with brute force, but we need to catch them off guard. We need something they won't see coming."

A hush fell over the tapping and chewing. "Like what?"

"Maybe... a diversion." My thoughts were scattered, but a vague idea formed. "We could create a false threat somewhere far from where they're keeping Scarlett. While their forces are focused on that, I could slip in and get her out."

"Interesting idea," his tapping started up again, "although they may be expecting something like that."

I clenched my teeth as he repeated my own doubts to me. I already knew they would probably expect a diversion, but with me going in after her without a gang of my own, I needed one.

"I can create some digital chaos, make it seem like a rival gang is attacking them," Phantom said, easing some tension in my body. "Or I could even create a blackout."

Though I knew he couldn't see it, I nodded, my chest tightening against the weight of our reality. "But we need to act fast. The longer she stays with them, the more at risk she becomes."

"Understood. I've gotten access to the security cameras now. It may take a while to comb through everything, but I'll find her, Boss. I swear."

CHAPTER 33

The Survivor

A throbbing pain pulsed behind my eyes as I slowly regained consciousness. The cold, icy ground pressed against my back served as an unwelcome reminder that I was no longer in the warmth and comfort of the cabin. I blinked several times, trying to clear the fog from my vision. As my eyes adjusted to the dim lighting, I realized I was in some kind of warehouse. Stacked crates and rusty shelves lined the perimeter, while a single dangling light bulb illuminated the vast empty space in the center. I was in a small room, lying on a concrete floor with my hands tied behind my back, the rough rope biting into my wrists.

Trying to sit up, I winced as sharp pains radiated through my ribs and shoulder. The pain only worsened my racing heart. Fear coursed through me as the memories came rushing back—the SUV, the chloroform-soaked rag over my mouth. They'd kidnapped me.

My thoughts drifted back to the chaos of that night—the armed men storming into the cabin, Bane yelling at me to run before they descended on him. I never even had a chance to get away. He tried to protect me, but we were outnumbered.

The thought of him caused an ache in my chest that threatened to break me. Being alone and at the mercy of my abductors, I did not know whether he was alive or dead. There was no way of knowing if he would come for me, or if I would ever see him again.

I took a deep breath, trying to slow down my racing heart, needing to keep calm so I could think. Wriggling my hands, I felt along the knotted ropes, searching for weakness. The fibers were tight but slightly frayed. If I could find something sharp...

Scanning the room, I spotted a rusted nail jutting out of a wooden crate in the corner. I dropped to the floor and scooted along the floor, maneuvering myself until the nail was within reach. With my hands twisted around me, I worked the rope back and forth over the sharp metal, continuing even as it scratched my skin.

Come on, come on.

Gritting my teeth, I sawed faster. After what felt like an eternity, the ropes split and my hands broke free. I wasted no time dropping to the floor and untying the bonds around my ankles.

With a deep breath, I tried to push down the panic rising in my chest. No matter how afraid I was, I couldn't show it to them. With my husband, I learned that lesson the hard way. For me to find a way out of the situation I was in, I had to stay strong. Despite everything I'd been through, I was a survivor, and I would never let myself become a victim ever again.

As tears burned the backs of my eyes, I clung to the memory of Bane, *of Ethan*, telling me that I was stronger than I thought. There was no way I would let him down.

I rose to my feet, determination sweeping through me. I needed to get out of there, so although I had no idea what they wanted from me, I had no intention of making it easy for them.

Creeping toward the door, I pressed my ear against the cold metal, listening as muffled voices drifted from the other side.

"The Boss wants her in one piece for negotiations. We can't afford any screw ups," a man said, the gruff, accented voice sending a chill down my spine and turning my blood to ice.

"Relax, we got this covered. Ain't no way she's getting past us," said another man in reply.

Pressing my ear to the door again although I wanted to hide, I strained to hear more.

"Mr. Delacroix wants the girl unharmed. He has plans for her," the gruff voice added.

The moment the name Delacroix met my ears, my breath became stuck in my throat, my chest too tight for my lungs to expand. I knew that name. My father had an old business partner by the same name before they had a major falling out. I wasn't sure why they'd stopped working together, and I wasn't sure what Delacroix wanted with me.

My mind raced, trying to connect the dots, wondering if Delacroix was somehow connected to Joshua. It couldn't have been a coincidence. If he was tied to Joshua, I didn't understand why Joshua hadn't walked into the room yet and terrorized me for running out on him. No matter what he'd done to me, he would still blame me, and he wouldn't allow me to be there for a second before he barged in to gloat and punish me himself.

The other thought that tumbled into my mind, as I listened to the men speak of me as though I was nothing more than an object, was if they were trying to use me as leverage against my father. Since I barely spoke to my father, I had no way of knowing. If there was beef between my father and Delacroix, I had no idea what that could possibly be, but it was the most likely possibility.

Turning around and leaning my back against the door, I swallowed, fear burning its way up my esophagus. Whether Delacroix was connected to Joshua or my father, one thing was clear. They planned to use me as leverage. Against my own father. Against my husband. Either way, I had to get out of there, but the door was solid steel. There was no way I could break it down.

The reality of my situation flooded my blood with panic. I pulled away from the cool metal of the door, lungs struggling for breath as I searched the room for anything I could use to pick the lock or pry it open, but approaching footsteps forced me back to where I was tied up. I haphazardly wrapped the bindings back around my limbs, hoping whoever came in didn't notice I had cut them free.

A heartbeat later, the heavy door screeched open, spilling harsh fluorescent light into the dim room. A hulking silhouette filled the doorway, features obscured in the shadows. As he stepped inside, the overhead bulb flickered on, illuminating the face of Victor Delacroix.

"Surprised to see me, Scarlett?"

A shudder trickled through my body as Victor's lips curled into a cruel smirk. For nearly my entire life, Victor was one of my father's business associates, a constant dark presence lurking in the background of my childhood. I thought I'd left his sinister gaze behind me when I broke from my father's world, but there he was in front of me, just as menacing as always.

"What the hell do you want from me?" I demanded, forcing more power into my voice than I truly felt, unwilling to let him see how much his presence unnerved me.

The chuckle that came out of his mouth turned my stomach. "Straight to business then... just like your father." As he prowled closer, it took everything in me to resist the urge to back away. "You're going to help convince Daddy Dearest to come out of retirement. We've got some unfinished business—expensive business—he and I."

"My father?" I stared at him in confusion. My father wasn't retired at all—at least not from his finance company. "I haven't spoken to my father in forever. I don't have any sway over what he does."

His eyes turned cold, the amusement vanishing. "Oh, I think you'll change your tune when you hear what I've got to say about him. Your dear old dad has been keeping secrets from you, Scarlett. Even if you haven't spoken to him in years, it may be time you do."

My heart pounded, but I lifted my chin in defiance. "I don't care what lies you're spinning. Even if we don't have the closest relationship, there's nothing you can say that will make me turn on my father."

Tsking, Victor's mouth twisted into a cruel grin. "So, you approve of your father's dirty business dealings? His crimes? You approve of how you were nothing but a pawn he placed directly in Joshua Prejean's hands?"

I froze, shock coursing through me. *No.* It couldn't have been true. My father would never... Even as I shook my head, however, trying to deny it, a creeping sense of doubt was worming its way into my mind.

"Oh yes," Victor purred. "Your father knew exactly the kind of man Joshua was, but the financial benefits of the alliance were too great, and your daddy is greedy, so he arranged that first meeting between the two of you. Your entire marriage was orchestrated by the men in your life. None of it was real."

Part of me was skeptical to believe anything Victor said, but I still felt like I'd been punched in the gut. I knew my father knew Joshua before he met me, but I'd never imagined...

Rage boiled up inside me, sending acid up my throat until I thought I may scream, but I tried to hide it in my expression. Even if my father had sold me to that monster—given me to him like an object to torture and abuse—I was still being held hostage, and I didn't understand why.

"You're lying," I hissed, but my voice shook. Deep down, I feared he was telling the truth. Too many things suddenly made terrible sense. My father's impatience with my unhappiness in the marriage and his insistence that I try harder to make it work was why we'd stopped speaking. It was never about me or Joshua at all. It was just about money. It was *always* about money with them.

There was suddenly another reason for me to escape. I had to confront my father and demand the truth.

Victor was watching me closely, gauging my reaction. Hoping he wouldn't see how deeply his revelation had cut me, I did my best to smooth my features into a mask.

Later. I would deal with it later. At that moment, I needed to stay focused. I needed to learn what I could and look for any chance to escape.

Shrugging as though I didn't care, I lifted my eyes to meet Victor's cold gaze. "Well, that's all ancient history now. What exactly do you expect me to do about it?"

Victor's eyes glinted, his smirk telling me he didn't buy my facade at all. "You'll find out soon enough, princess."

His smug expression made my skin crawl, but I hid my disgust behind the mask of indifference. If there was one thing I was good at, it was hiding my true feelings.

"So, what's next for me in this little melodrama?" I asked, keeping my tone bored. "More threats? Maybe demands for ransom? Really, this whole captivity thing is getting tedious."

Victor chuckled, reminding me of a television Mob Boss. "All in due time, my dear. For now, let's get you something to eat. You must be famished. "Lighting a cigar, he yelled over his shoulder. "Miguel! Bring in some food for our special guest."

Moments later, a young man entered through the open doorway, detaching himself from the shadows. Of all the hulking brutes holding me captive, I hadn't expected one so average looking. He kept his eyes downcast as he approached, his dark curls falling over his forehead. His slender frame looked out of place among Victor's thugs. "Here," he mumbled, handing me a plate of eggs and toast, his fingers trembling as they brushed against mine. Our eyes met for an instant before he looked away. But in that moment, I glimpsed the fear in his gaze, and something more. *Compassion.*

Perhaps I had found my one potential ally among the criminals who'd beaten the man I loved and kidnapped me, but I realized it would be dangerous to trust anyone in that warehouse. Still, I couldn't help wondering if Miguel could be the key to my escape.

CHAPTER 34

The Savior

As I waited for Phantom to gather more information, I paced my apartment, my thoughts consumed by Scarlett's plight and how it was my fault. She could be anywhere, and I had no way to find her until Phantom hacked into the security cameras along the route and told me what direction they'd gone. Images of her haunted me—her dark brown eyes filled with fear—her once-strong spirit broken by the monsters who were holding her captive. I couldn't shake the feeling that time was running out, and the thought of losing her drove me to the brink of desperation.

Fury coursing through my veins as much at myself as at the assholes who'd taken her, I slammed my fist into the wall of my office. Plaster and drywall exploded from the impact, wooden shards splitting my knuckles. The pain was only a fraction of the agony in my chest. Just as I swung my arm back to hit it again, my phone vibrated in my pocket.

Heart hammering against my ribcage, I answered the phone before the second ring. "Anything yet?"

"Not yet, Boss. But I'm digging through everything. Traffic cams, security feeds, encrypted messages... you name it. If there's a digital trail, I'll find it. I'll find her. It's just a lot of files."

It took everything in me not to fall to my knees from the blow. Scarlett had already been gone more than a day and that was a day too long.

"Hey, open up your email and check this out," he said, excitement seeping into his voice as his fingers clicked on his keyboard. "This email chain between Joshua and Victor Delacroix—looks like they've been in cahoots for some time now."

"Victor Delacroix?" My eyes narrowed, more rage simmering beneath the surface. He was the head of a rival Mob organization, and his name carried a lot of weight in the criminal underworld.

"Yep," Phantom confirmed. "It seems Joshua's been receiving payments from Victor in exchange for certain... *favors*."

"Damn it," I muttered under my breath, grabbing a rag out of the kitchen and wrapping it around my fist that had begun to seep blood on my keyboard.

"Boss, there's more," Phantom added, his tone turning serious. "Based on these communications, it looks like Scarlett's kidnapping is part of a bigger plan orchestrated by Victor. He's using her as leverage to get what he wants from Ivy. I've accessed files on Joshua's numerous shady business deals, and pieced together a web of illegal activities, from money laundering to drug trafficking. It appears that Scarlett is just caught in the middle."

His words sent a chill down my spine, and my grip on the mouse tightened. To think that Scarlett was caught up in such schemes sickened me. Unlike them, and unlike me, Scarlett was good and had an innocent heart. She didn't deserve anything she was going through.

Running my fingers through my hair, I blew out a breath, trying to calm my rage. Scarlett needed my actions, not my emotions. My only advantage, or at least I hoped was still the case, was that Victor's men didn't know I was still alive, and they didn't know my true identity. If they did, I had no doubts they would have already kicked the door down of my apartment. The fact that they hadn't told me that I was still an unknown to them. That was something I could use.

"Phantom, we need to act fast. These people are ruthless." The urgency flooding through my veins rushed like a tsunami behind my eardrums, the need to run out into the city and tear it apart to find her testing my sanity. If I went out there without a plan, I knew I could get her killed, so although I needed to do something—*anything*—to get to her, I stood from my desk and returned to my weapons, making sure my magazines were filled. Just because I couldn't find and shoot Victor yet didn't mean I couldn't shoot something. If I didn't get answers soon, someone would find my gun against their temple until they told me what I needed to know.

"Get everything you can on Victor and his organization. I also need to get to a safehouse—somewhere I can bring Scarlett once I find her." For a moment, my thoughts went to my sister and niece, who were unknowingly in danger in the hospital. The hospital had security, but if the Mob discovered who I really was... I pushed the thought away, my mind much too panicked to add more onto my plate. In the meantime, all I could do was hire someone to watch over them and give my sister a head's up. I'd done it before when dealing with powerful people, so I knew exactly who to call.

Phantom hummed as he worked on his laptop for a few minutes, my mind so busy I barely paid attention. When he did clear his throat, the sound coming through the earpiece I'd nearly forgotten was in my ear, my head jerked up with how wired up I was. "Understood, Boss. Do you need me to find you a safehouse, or do you have somewhere in mind?"

As he waited for an answer, I darted back into my office, scrolling through documents on my laptop to make sure what I was looking for was still available. "No, I've got somewhere I can go. I just need to get some things packed up and squared away. What's most important is finding Scarlett."

"Absolutely, Bane, but we've dug up something big. From the documents I've hacked into on Ivy's end, it appears as though there was a falling out with Victor and Ivy many years ago, and Joshua's alliance with Victor may be what triggered the hit Ivy put out on Joshua. It's basically a gang war, although Ivy's involvement has definitely lessened over the past year."

My mind raced, trying to process the tangled web of deceit and betrayal Scarlett had been unknowingly ensnared in. It was no wonder she was so guarded, so closed off. The people who were supposed to love her were using her as a pawn in their twisted games, and although she didn't seem to know all the facts, she still felt the backlash of their feud.

"Phantom, we need to learn more about who is in Victor's gang and where they are holding up," I said, my voice hard. "If I can track down one of his men, I can get information out of him."

"Okay." The sound of rapid keystrokes accompanied Phantom's words, the tapping driving up my heart rate. "Let me see what else I can dig up on Victor's organization, and we'll devise our strategy from there."

Two more hours passed while I waited for Phantom to get back to me. Unable to pace any longer, and having scoured through the documents he'd sent me multiple times, setting up a bodyguard for my sister, and then contacting my sister to argue with her about it, I finally nodded off on the sofa when my phone notified me of a call.

"Got some fresh intel for you, Boss." Phantom's voice crackled over the phone as I stood and leaned against the wall, my muscles twitching with the need to do something useful to get my Little Red back. "It seems Victor has a few key players in his organization who are crucial to his operations, but there are plenty who do the grunt work. They may be your way in."

"Send me everything you've got," I said, my fingers gripping the phone tightly. Phantom had never let me down before, and I knew he wouldn't start now, but my patience was still waning.

"Check your email. It's all there." Although I thought I understood what he'd said, the sound of him munching on chips made it difficult to translate. I rolled my eyes. Despite the gravity of the situation, Phantom's casual demeanor was oddly comforting.

"Thanks," I muttered, ending the call and pulling up the secured email on my laptop. The information flashed across the screen, and my eyes scanned through it at lightning speed. The bastards were going down, one way or another, but the sooner I found them, the better.

Studying the photographs and profiles Phantom provided, I committed each face and detail to memory. They were low-level thugs, but they were still dangerous—especially in numbers. I needed a plan that would allow me to get close without putting Scarlett at risk, and I had no qualms about torturing a few of Victor's men to do it.

Tapping my fingers against my thigh in frustration, I searched through the names and details again, my eyes straining from my exhaustion. Images of Scarlett's gentle smile and her dark brown eyes haunted me, spurring me to find a solution, even as my body threatened to shut down from going so long injured and with no sleep.

"Gotcha," I murmured as my gaze locked onto one member of the gang. *My target.* He was young, inexperienced, and most importantly, due to make a solo pickup later tonight. That, in itself, made it my best chance. I intended to track him down and get what I needed from him. With any luck, he would lead me straight to Scarlett.

"Time for a visit, kid," I said under my breath, my determination hardening into an icy resolve. I might have been a cold-blooded killer, but my Little Red's warmth had started to thaw my frozen heart, and I would do whatever it took to ensure her safety.

As I slipped on my gloves and grabbed my weapons, a single thought echoed through my mind: Victor Delacroix's gang would soon learn that they had messed with the wrong man... and the wrong woman. Scarlett was a survivor, and I would always be the monster hiding in the shadows and slaying her dragons for her, even though we both knew she could slay them herself.

CHAPTER 35

The Survivor

The sun had barely risen above the horizon when I jolted awake, not sure what day it was, my heart hammering against my bruised rib cage when the dim light filtering through the dusty windows of the warehouse reminded me of where I was. After Victor and Miguel had left, I'd stared at the walls until I'd fallen asleep, with nothing more than my thoughts and the sound of footsteps outside the door to keep me company.

The shadows clung to the corners of the small room like cobwebs. Hugging my knees to my chest, I shivered against the damp cold that seeped through the concrete walls. My body ached, bruises mottling my arms and legs. I ran my fingers over the raw skin on my wrists, chafed from the ropes they'd used to bind me. My throat burned, dry and cracked from lack of water. They kept me weak, just strong enough to stay alive, but too feeble to fight back.

Needing a respite, I squeezed my eyes shut, but the darkness behind my eyelids was no escape. Flashes of memory played like a slideshow of nightmares—the van screeching up beside me, rough hands dragging me inside, the blindfold cinched so tight I saw stars.

"Please..." My voice scraped against the rawness in my throat. "Please just let me go."

Only the echoes of my plea answered back. I was alone. No one knew where I was, and no one was coming to save me.

Despair pressed down with such weight I could barely breathe. What was the point in fighting anymore? They had won. My spirit was broken, shattered beyond repair like rays of light swallowed up in this endless gloom.

I bowed my head, tears burning trails down my cheeks. How much more could I endure before the last flicker of hope inside me finally went out? Although I'd convinced myself that I was a survivor, being held captive in such conditions only forced me back into the submissive woman I was with Joshua. I didn't know how to fight when I knew I would lose.

The heavy door creaked open, casting a sliver of light into the dark room. I flinched at the sudden brightness, squinting to make out the two figures standing before me.

"Well, well. Look who's awake," one of them sneered. I recognized the gruff voice of the man who'd grabbed me first.

The other man gave a sinister chuckle. "Sleep well, princess?"

Turning my eyes downward, I didn't respond. I knew better than to talk back. When they approached me from the doorway, I glanced up at them through my eyelashes, their amused glances at each other numbing my limbs. I was petrified of what they could do to me, but I didn't know how to prevent it. "Seems your dear Bane hasn't come to rescue you after all," the first man said. "Guess you're not as important to him as you thought."

My head snapped up at the mention of Bane's name, a cold dread seeping through me.

The second man laughed, the sound inhumanly cruel. "Oh yes, we know all about your boyfriend. But you don't need to worry about him anymore." He paused, his smile growing wider. "Because he's dead."

"What?" The word tore from my throat before I could stop it, the need to vomit warring with my need to deny their claim. There was no way I could live in a word he didn't exist in, not anymore.

"Took care of him ourselves," the first man said, smug pride twisting his gruff features. "He's at the bottom of the river by now."

Even as I shook my head, my heart wrenched open, refusing to believe it was true, but the satisfied gleam in their eyes told me they weren't lying.

A ragged breath escaped me as my chest constricted. Bile burned its way up my throat, forcing me to double over as it made its way onto the floor. Bane, my protector, the man I loved, was gone. The grief hit me like a physical blow, the punch to my gut forcing me to retch more as sobs wracked my body.

Through the haze of tears, I heard their laughter and saw their blurry outlines leaving the room. They'd accomplished what they came there to do. Physical torture would have been a kindness compared to what they were putting me through, and they knew that.

As I curled up on the concrete floor, begging for the oblivion of death, the door slammed shut behind them, enveloping me in darkness once more. Once I was alone again, I pulled myself up to sit, wrapping my arms around my knees and pressing my back into the cold, damp wall. The chill seeped through my thin shirt, raising goosebumps on my skin, but I barely felt a thing. Instead, I wept until I had no tears left. I didn't know how to go on without Bane, but I knew I had to find a way even if I didn't want to. *For him.*

Hours passed as I sat there, the room so quiet I could hear my own ragged breathing. Outside, rain pattered against the small warehouse window, the only reminder that a world existed beyond my prison cell.

Inhaling deeply, I took in the musty scent of mold and mildew that permeated the air. My thoughts drifted to Bane—*to Ethan*, conjuring his face in my mind's eye. His piercing blue eyes that saw straight through to my soul, his rough but gentle hands that made me feel so safe—that pleasured me like none ever had before, and the warmth of his smile that he reserved only for me.

My heart shattered all over again at the realization I would never see his smile again, never feel the comfort of his embrace. A choked sob escaped my throat as the despair set in, but I swiped angrily at the tears staining my cheeks. If I was going to survive this, I had to be strong. I had to fight. For myself and for Bane's memory.

Taking a deep breath, I lifted my head, refusing to let them break me. I slowly uncurled from my huddled position, wincing as my bruised body protested. Moving hurt but staying still hurt more. If I kept lying there and drowning in my sorrow, I would lose the last thread of my sanity. Once I was no longer in Victor's clutches, then I could lose my mind. I couldn't give him the satisfaction of taking that too.

With the little strength I had left, I forced myself to stand on shaky legs, stumbling to the door. As expected, it was locked tight. I banged my palm against it in frustration, the dull thud echoing through the small room.

308

"Let me out!" I screamed, not surprised there was no response. I was alone.

Exhausted, I slid down the door and sat on the cold concrete floor. I thought of Ethan again, imagining his deep voice telling me I was stronger than I knew. A sad smile touched my lips as a few more tears escaped. No matter what those men had said, I had to believe I would find a way back to him. He couldn't truly be gone. My heart refused to accept it.

Taking a deep breath, I straightened my shoulders, gathering my resolve. Slowly, methodically, I examined every inch of the room, looking for any weakness, anything I could use when my eyes finally landed on the metal bed frame in the corner.

Wasting no time, I rose to my feet, crossing the room and ripping off a bar with all my strength, grunting from the effort. The end was jagged where it had broken off, reminding me of a piece of rebar. It wasn't a gun or a knife, but I could still do damage with it.

A wicked smile crawled across my lips, the weapon in my hands giving me strength I didn't have before. My captors thought they'd broken me, but they were wrong. I was stronger than they realized, and I would do whatever it took to get back to Bane.

Gripping the metal bar like a sword, I pressed my back to the wall by the door. If I was going to survive, it was time to fight.

Footsteps approached the door from outside, a man with a thick Cajun accent greeting whoever was guarding my door. My fingers wrapped around the bar until my fingers went numb as I listened to their conversation.

"You really think this'll work?" the first man asked, his voice getting louder as he leaned against the wall near the door. "Using her as leverage against her father?"

"Of course," the second man scoffed. "He's got no choice but to cooperate if he wants to save his precious daughter. Victor knows what he's doing."

"Her father has made some powerful enemies," the first man continued. "Once word gets out that we've got her, they'll all be clamoring for a piece, and we'll be sitting pretty at the top whether Ivy pays up or not."

"Exactly," the second one responded. "And with her in our possession, there's no way he can touch us. It's a win-win situation."

As I listened to their exchange, my mind raced with conflicting emotions. On the one hand, I was furious at my father for putting me in this dangerous position. I couldn't imagine what Victor wanted from him that was worth what they were doing to me. On the other hand, I wanted to protect my father. He may have been shady, but he was the only father I would ever have.

Pushing my thoughts aside, I continued to eavesdrop on their conversation, praying that they would reveal some crucial detail or weakness that could help me escape.

"Delacroix is bringing some of his top guys with him when he comes back tonight," the first man said, sounding almost impressed. "He said we should be ready to move her in a couple of days."

"Good. The sooner we get this over with, the better," replied his companion, the impatience evident in his tone. "We can't afford any more screw-ups."

With each passing moment, my resolve grew stronger, fueled by the knowledge that my survival—and that of my father—depended on my ability to outsmart these dangerous men. Despite the odds stacked against me, I refused to back down, but as the hours dragged on and my captors' conversation grew increasingly mundane, I couldn't help but feel a sense of desperation creeping in. Time was running out, and I still had no clear path to freedom and no idea what they were trying to get out of my father.

CHAPTER 36

The Savior

As night fell, I positioned myself on a rooftop over-looking the meeting spot. The young gang member, Vinnie, was supposed to make the drop off any minute. My pulse thrummed with anticipation, but I remained patient and focused. Despite my growing feelings for Scarlett, I couldn't let emotion cloud my judgment, not when so much was at stake.

The sound of an approaching car broke through my thoughts, only heightening my senses. Peering over the edge of the rooftop, I watched as Vinnie stepped out of his vehicle and glanced around nervously, his frame tall and lanky. It was clear he wasn't used to operating alone. *Perfect.* The person he was there to meet was already inside, having parked on the other side of the building, but I wasn't concerned about him. He would never even know I was there. I, on the other hand, had already cased the area and prepped the dilapidated structure to go up in flames when I was finished with it. If I wanted to create a distraction, setting fire to a building where their guy was doing a drop would certainly work.

As Vinnie walked away from his car, I climbed down the fire escape, trailing him from enough of a distance to ensure I remained undetected. Since I knew where he was headed, I remained outside for a moment, allowing him to get a head start inside.

In the darkened night, the abandoned building loomed ominously before me, its once-elegant façade now marred by graffiti and decay. Broken windows stared back at me like empty eye sockets, and the wind moaned through the cracks in the walls, making eerie sounds across the parking lot. Rain fell in gentle sheets, adding to the haunting atmosphere. The place reeked of danger, sending a shiver of unease down my spine, but there was nothing that could keep me from going in after him. He was my way to Scarlett.

Once entering the building, I navigated through the dark, narrow corridors, my footsteps muffled by layers of dust and grime, and the storm increasing in intensity outside. I didn't see the kid in front of me, but the footprints on the ground told me which direction to go.

Cobwebs stretched across the rooms like sinister veils, their occupants long gone, leaving behind only the ghosts. The air felt heavy, as if it carried the weight of countless secrets and crimes that had taken place within the crumbling walls. There would be another one to add to the roster on this night, but not until I got a little information out of Vinnie first.

As I crept through the long-abandoned building, I couldn't help but think of Scarlett—how she had touched something inside me and made me feel alive again. No matter what I had to do, no matter who I had to kill, I would save my Little Red. There was no question.

Seeing the beam of a flashlight in the open room ahead, I crouched in the shadows, watching Vinnie from a distance. The muscles in my legs tensed, ready to spring into action when the opportunity presented itself. I knew I had to be patient, biding my time until the moment was right.

"Hey, Vinnie!" a voice called out from within the darkness, causing me to tense, but as I peered forward, I could see the shadow of the other man who was already in the room with him. "You got the goods?"

"As ordered," Vinnie responded, his voice echoing off the crumbling walls. "Let's get on with it. This place is creepy. I heard it's haunted.

The other guy chuckled, his steps moving farther away from me. "You know I'll have to count it first.

"Alright, alright." Vinnie sighed, the sound heavy with annoyance. While he was worried about ghosts, he was completely oblivious to the fact that he was being hunted by someone who was very much alive.

For several minutes, they didn't speak as the other man counted whatever was in the package. I waited in the dark room off the corridor, hoping to get Vinnie alone once they were finished conducting their business.

"Alright," the other man finally said, his feet shuffling on the concrete. "You're good to go, Vinnie. Until next time."

On silent feet, I moved back down the corridor, hiding in the darkness behind Vinnie's vehicle. The moonlit night seemed to be holding its breath as I navigated through the shadows, careful not to make any sound.

When my target stepped out of the derelict building, I saw my chance. A single beam of light illuminated his figure, giving me just enough cover as I silently advanced on him. My breathing slowed, mind sharpening as every detail became crucial.

As soon as he was within reach, I lunged at him with the full force of my body. Before he could react, my arm snaked around his neck, cutting off his air supply. His hands clawed futilely at my arm, but I held on tight, my grip unyielding.

"Sorry, buddy," I muttered into his ear, my voice cold and detached. "But I need information, and you're going to give it to me."

His struggles grew weaker, his strength waning as the lack of oxygen took its toll. As he lost consciousness, I hoisted his limp body over my shoulder and carried him back to the abandoned building, waiting until the other man walked away before I entered through a different door.

"Time to face your demons," I told Vinnie's unconscious form as I dropped him into a chair, gagged him, and then bound him securely with zip ties. I placed my flashlight on the ground pointing at the exposed rafters above, creating ominous shadows on the graffiti-strewn walls.

Vinnie's eyes flickered open as I cracked open smelling salts beneath his nostrils, confusion and fear evident in his gaze when he caught sight of me standing in front of him with my arms crossed and an icy expression on my face.

"Good evening, Vinnie," I said, flipping another chair around so I could straddle it. "Welcome to your own personal hell."

Eyes widening into disks, he struggled against his restraints, but his efforts were futile. Panic set in as he tried to scream through the gag and realized I was the only person who could hear him.

"Let's get straight to the point, shall we?" I continued, my voice devoid of emotion. "You're going to tell me everything you know about Victor Delacroix's gang and where they're holding my girl. And if you don't ... Well, let's just say things will get *very* unpleasant for you. And don't bother screaming, Vinnie. Your friend is already miles away by now."

He mumbled something through the gag, his body squirming until he nearly flipped the entire chair over. Kicking the chair back into place, I removed the gag, allowing him to speak. "I don't know what you're talking about, man! I swear!"

"Wrong answer." I slid brass knuckles onto my hand. Without another word, I struck, the brass knuckles splitting his face open.

He cried out, thrashing on the chair and nearly flipping it over again. "I don't know anything, man!"

With a shake of my head, I hit him again, the bones in his nose giving way with a sickening crunch. "Wrong answer again, Vinnie."

For a moment, I thought he would speak, but all he did was cry like a little punk. Giving him one more bored look, I walked over to a rickety table and retrieved a pair of pliers. Seeing the instrument of his potential torment in my hands, Vinnie's eyes blew wider.

"Wait! *Please*, man! Oh, god, wait! I'll talk! I'll talk!"

"Start talking," I barked, my gaze never leaving his as I twirled the tool in my fingers. "I'm losing my patience, Vinnie. I have places to be."

"Alright! Alright! Victor's got some big plan in the works." Words tumbled out of his mouth like vomit, sweat beading on his forehead. "Something about a shipment coming in. I don't know all the details, but Ivy Etienne's gang broke off an agreement with Victor when Ivy stepped down and Victor's pissed about it. Ivy's daughter is being held at an old distillery near the river to force her father's hand."

"Go on," I pressed, stepping closer to him with the pliers still in my hand. "Who's guarding her? How many men?"

"Uh... I think there's like five, maybe six guys." His voice stammered, his eyes following my every move. "I swear, that's all I know!"

Remaining silent for a moment, I studied his face, searching for any flicker of deceit. It was clear he was scared, but I had to be sure his information was reliable. One wrong move could put Scarlett in even greater danger.

"Vinnie," I said, taking another step toward him. "I need you to think *very* carefully about what you just told me. Any inconsistencies or lies could mean the difference between life and death—for my girl, and for yourself."

"Okay, okay!" Vinnie swallowed hard, his face reddening as his breathing grew ragged. "Like I said, there's a shipment coming in—some kind of big deal. Victor's got it all planned out. It's happening tomorrow night. And yeah, she's at that distillery on the east side. But that's really all I know! I swear!"

"Who else knows about the shipment?"

"Uh... some of the higher-ups in the gang, I guess? I don't know their names, man! We're not exactly on a first-name basis. Look, I don't know! I'm just a courier." Vinnie cried out in frustration, his arms yanking on the zip ties until they started to bleed. "I'm not one of them, man! I'm just a low-level guy!"

"Good," I said, satisfied with the information he'd provided. There were only so many distilleries in the city, so I knew where to look. "You just bought yourself a one-way ticket out of this nightmare."

"Please, let me go," he pleaded, his fear palpable as I stepped back toward the table. "I won't tell anyone about this, I promise!"

Turning my back on him, I slipped the pliers into my pocket and pulled out my knife, sliding my finger along the blade. "Unfortunately, Vinnie, loose ends have a habit of unraveling."

CHAPTER 37

The Survivor

After at least an hour of listening to the two men, I found myself pacing the dimly lit room, my rapid heart rate making it impossible to sit down. The overwhelming sense of urgency clawed at me, leaving me breathless and on edge—ready to gouge my way out of the room with my fingernails.

As I paced, trying to get my energy out in any way I could, footsteps approached the door, sending my heart into my throat.

Returning to the door, I pressed my back against the wall and braced myself for whatever was to come. For a moment, time seemed to stand still, my breath seizing in my chest as though my body didn't want them to hear me.

When the door swung open, a burly man walked in, his face hidden in shadows as he tossed a sandwich wrapped in plastic wrap onto the floor. "Eat up, bitch. You'll need your strength for what's coming."

As he turned to leave, adrenaline flooded through my veins, giving me strength I didn't know I had. Without a thought, I seized the opportunity and lunged forward. In one swift motion, I swung the bar in my hand, smashing it into his forehead. He collapsed to the ground with a heavy thud.

Taking a deep breath to steady my nerves, I stepped over his unconscious body, the metal bar heavy in my sweaty palm. I didn't know what I was doing. I had never attacked anyone in my life, but instinct controlled me, giving me no choice. With one more deep breath, I moved toward the doorway.

Listening for voices nearby and not hearing anyone, I poked my head out the door, peering down the dim hallway and was relieved when it was empty. On silent feet, I slipped out of the room, sliding the door closed and sticking close to the wall. All I needed was to find a way out of the maze of corridors.

My mind was still reeling from the conversation I'd overheard, wondering what my father could have done to get on the wrong side of Victor Delacroix and his Mob connections. I knew he had made some bad investments in the past, but I couldn't imagine him being involved in something so dangerous. I still didn't know how Joshua fit into the situation, but I knew he did.

Although Joshua's involvement didn't surprise me, the thought of my father being involved in organized crime made my heart ache. I didn't want to believe it, but the evidence was stacking up against him. Had he known about Joshua's criminal activities when he'd encouraged me to marry him? Had it all been part of some twisted plan? Those were questions I didn't know the answers to, and the potential answers brought acid up my throat. I swallowed hard, forcing the thoughts away. Until I was free, I couldn't deal with any of it. My sole focus needed to be on getting out of here alive.

As I crept down the first corridor and to the next, voices echoed from around a corner up ahead. Ice flooded my veins and I froze, pressing myself back against the wall, my pulse roaring in my ears. There was no doubt that if they found me out of my room, I was as good as dead. I held my breath, straining to hear the approaching voices.

"The Boss wants her kept under a twenty-four-hour watch," one man said, the same man with the gruff voice. "We can't afford any screw ups."

"Relax, she's not going anywhere," another scoffed. "Little Miss Priss is too scared to make a move."

Their laughter turned my stomach. I searched the area around me for somewhere to hide when I saw a supply closet ajar just a few feet away. As their footsteps drew nearer, I slipped inside, pulling the door nearly closed behind me.

Through the crack, I watched two hulking men stride past, dressed in dark suits with guns holstered at their hips. They were so close, I could smell the cigarette smoke on their breath.

Once their footsteps faded, I sagged back against the shelves, blowing out a shaky breath. Delacroix's men were everywhere, watching my every move, making it nearly impossible for me to get away.

After several moments of sheer panic, I left the relative safety of the closet and crept down the hallway, keeping to the shadows as I strained to hear any sign of the guards. Up ahead, an ornate mahogany door stood slightly ajar, warm light spilling out into the corridor. I paused in a shadowed alcove, listening as a man's smooth baritone voice drifted out, sending a chill down my spine.

"...the exchange will happen tomorrow. No mistakes."

"Bring the girl once we have the documents," Delacroix continued. "Her father will pay any price when he sees the photos."

My stomach dropped. If they hadn't taken photos yet, I knew they were going to find me missing as soon as they went to take them. When they found my room empty, escape would go from improbable to impossible.

Delacroix kept talking, but I could barely focus through the roaring in my ears. I had to get out of there—*immediately—before* they found me missing.

With trembling hands, I crept away from Delacroix's office. Claustrophobia made my skin tingle, the windowless hallways like a tomb closing in around me. Doing my best to ignore my fear, I kept moving through the maze of corridors, sticking to the shadows. My pulse pounded as I slipped past mobsters standing guard, knowing one wrong move and I would be dead.

Finally, I spotted it—a door that had to lead outside—hanging open as someone outside smoked a cigarette. Heart leaping, I peered through the crack to see a loading dock, leading out to a quiet side street. It was my way out, if only I could get there unnoticed.

Waiting until the nearest guard turned his back, I darted forward, my bare feet silent on the concrete floor. I was steps away from freedom when—

"Hey!" A shout rang out behind me, forcing me to stumble. "Where do you think you're going?"

With my jaw clenched, I turned to face the angry guard storming toward me, one hand reaching for his radio to raise the alarm. As he got close, I exploded into motion, my elbow smashing into his nose with a sickening crunch. Before he could recover, I grabbed his radio and pistol, sprinting for the exit.

Freedom was just steps away as I lunged for the door, only to find myself staring down the barrel of Victor's revolver, the weapons in my hand slapped to the floor.

"Nice try, princess," he sneered, pointing to the men closing in behind me. "But did you really think it would be that easy?"

My heart sank into the ground beneath my feet, but I lifted my chin in defiance. I glared at Victor, refusing to show the fear churning inside me.

"That was a very stupid thing to do," Victor said, his gun aimed at my chest. "You're lucky I don't put a bullet in you right now."

My mind raced, assessing my options. The gun was only a few feet away—if I could get to it, I might have had a chance. I tensed my muscles, preparing to dive.

Victor seemed to read my intention, pressing the gun forward until it was only inches from my head. "Don't even think about it," he warned. "On your knees. Now."

With no choice, I slowly sank to the concrete floor, my skin crawling at the forced submission. Victor grabbed my arm and wrenched me forward, shoving me toward his men.

"Tie her up," he ordered. "And make sure it's tight this time. No more chances."

Rough hands seized me, binding my wrists and ankles with coarse rope. I bit back a cry as the fibers dug into my abraded skin. Once I was secured, Victor grabbed my chin, forcing me to look at him.

"Your little escape attempt changes things," he said, his voice ice cold. "I wanted to use you as leverage with your father. But now..." His eyes hardened, filling me with dread. "Now you're nothing but a liability."

CHAPTER 38

The Savior

S itting in my parked car in an alley near the distillery, I took a deep breath, trying to rein in the rage threatening to overwhelm me. My laptop sat on my lap as I waited for Phantom to send blueprints to me. I'd parked a few blocks away from the structure, and my window tint was dark enough no one would be able to see me inside, even if Victor's men were to venture down the street.

After taking care of the snitch, I'd set the warehouse ablaze and driven straight to the distillery. There was too much nervous energy inside me to return to my apartment and stew. If I was lucky, the fire would be a distraction for the police, and for the gang Vinnie belonged to, taking some of their attention away from Scarlett and my attempt to save her.

"Okay, I'm in." Phantom's voice pulled me from my thoughts, his signature tapping slowing as my eyes flicked back to the screen. "Looks like there's three main buildings, all interconnected, and a big central courtyard with just one access point. The building has been vacant for decades. How's it look from the outside?"

Tearing my eyes away from my computer again, I glanced back out into the darkened night, my muscles twitching with the need to get out of the car and find my Little Red. I needed to be prepared first, but I didn't want her with them any longer than she already had been. "Like all the other abandoned buildings in this city that should have been torn down ages ago—a magnet for nothing but rats and crack addicts." *And where the bodies are buried...* but I didn't say that aloud. It was the last thing I wanted to think about with my girl still inside.

As I returned my attention to the laptop, I brought up the blueprints and studied the layout of the property. My jaw clenched. It would be difficult to get in and out undetected, but not impossible. It was a fortress, but I'd infiltrated fortresses before.

"Any way to cut power to the security system?" I asked, double checking the magazine of my gun and sliding it back into its holster. "Even for a few minutes?"

As rain pounded the blacktop, I stared back out the window, listening to Phantom hum as he worked on his computer. The longer I sat in the car, the more difficult it was for me to focus on only one thing. "I might be able to trigger a temporary blackout, but they'll have backup generators kicking in fast. It won't give you more than about five minutes—if that."

My mind raced, calculating variables, weighing options, but at the end of the day, I needed to trust my instincts. It was risky, but it would have to work. I would make this right. I would tear New Orleans apart brick by brick if I had to. Delacroix's men would pay for taking Scarlett.

"Alright," I said, turning off the ignition and closing my laptop to slide it beneath the seat. "I'm going in, so give me a few minutes before you shut them down. It'll have to be enough."

The cool rain soaked my black hoodie as I slipped out of my car and into the darkness, each step deliberate. The dilapidated Mob hideout loomed before me like the monster it was, a decaying fortress of corruption and violence. Years of working in the shadows taught me to let my instincts guide me, but tension still tightened my chest. My sole mission was to find Scarlett and get her out of this hellhole, but I didn't know where she was or what shape she was in, and that made it impossible to approach the situation in my usual manner. The stakes were too high, as were my emotions, making it impossible to go in with a cool head.

With the rain making heavy splatters on the ground, my boots were silent against the concrete as I crept along the outer wall of the compound. The place was a crumbling relic, all peeling paint and rusting beams that groaned under their own weight. The brick was weather-beaten and in chunks on the ground.

In the distance, a door creaked open, echoing through the night. The snap of a cigarette lighter, a flare of flame, and the acrid scent of tobacco drifted my way a moment later. I pressed myself into the darkness, holding my breath as I peered around the corner. One of Victor's men was on a smoke break, and he was just the thing I needed to get into the building.

Under the cover of rain, I waited, counting the seconds, listening to the rhythmic inhale and exhale of nicotine. On the sixth puff, the exterior light above the door went out, telling me Phantom's temporary blackout had been successful. As the unsuspecting thug cussed under his breath and reached for the door handle, there was a wet gurgle, a thud, and then two hundred pounds of dead weight hit the pavement by my feet.

The cigarette butt still glowed orange, a pinprick of light in the gloom, but I snuffed it under my heel and moved on. With no camera watching my movements, I slid into the building, disappearing into the pitch-black corridor.

Moving through the distillery like a ghost, I used the darkness as cover. The place was a maze of corridors and rooms filled with rusted machinery that stood like silent sentinels in the darkness, but I navigated it with ease, having memorized the layout before I'd gotten out of my car. I followed the mental map in my head, checking each corner before proceeding.

A scuffling sound up ahead met my ears and I froze, sinking into a doorway. Standing as still as a statue, I watched as a rat emerged from beneath a stack of crates, dragging its belly across the floor. It paused, beady eyes glinting in the half-light, and for a moment I thought it saw me before it skittered away down the hall. I exhaled, my fingers flexing on the hilt of my knife, the tension coiling tighter in my gut with each step. The compound seemed to stretch on forever, each turn leading to another grimy corridor filled with the stench of dust and mildew.

Edging forward, I slowed as voices met my ears from a larger chamber dimly lit by a single bulb swaying from the ceiling. The generator had kicked on, giving them light, but not much. The shadows welcomed me as an old friend as I circled the edge of the room. In the center, a card table had been set up, where three armed men played a game of poker, smoking and drinking from a bottle of whiskey. There was no sign of Scarlett, but I knew she couldn't have been far, not with her guards hanging out as though they had not a care in the world. The men were so engrossed in their game, chuckling and throwing insults at each other, that they were completely oblivious to the danger approaching.

One thug, bald and built like a linebacker, threw his cards down, rising from the table. My heart plummeted into my stomach as I waited for him to surge at me, but he turned back toward the hallway instead, yelling over his shoulder, "Forget this. I'll go check on the girl."

The urge to follow him nagged at me, but I forced myself to stay the course. Rushing in would only lead to mistakes, so I couldn't go after him until I got rid of his backup. Instead of following, I crouched behind a crate in the darkness, watching as he disappeared deeper into the building.

Once he was out of sight, I struck. My knife flashed, slicing through the first man's throat, blood spurting across the table. As his body crumpled, I grabbed the second man's head and twisted. His neck broke with a resounding crack, and he dropped to the ground like the garbage he was. I was pretty sure Victor wouldn't have been happy that his men were drinking and playing around on the job, but that wasn't my problem. He could deal with them when he met them in hell.

When the room fell silent, I wiped my knife on one of the men's shirts and trailed after baldy. He led me right to a locked room down one of the many empty corridors.

"Hey, sweetheart, you okay in there?" he called out with a chuckle. My blood boiled at his mocking tone, but I stayed focused, watching from just around the corner.

As he fished for his keys, I snuck up behind him, wrapping my arm around his neck and sliding my knife straight into the side of his throat, hitting his larynx and then yanking the knife toward his spinal cord. He struggled but went limp when the fatal strike hit his carotid artery and jugular vein. Straining under his weight, I lowered his body to the ground at my feet and then held my breath as I listened to make sure no one else was nearby.

With my heart sending blood crashing through my veins as the blood I'd drawn spilled onto the floor, I bent over and picked up baldy's keys. Sure no one else was coming, I slid them into the lock with trembling hands, pushing the heavy door open until I could peek inside.

In the center of the dark room, illuminated by the scant moonlight that came in through the dusty window, was my Little Red tied to a chair.

Scarlett.

CHAPTER 39

The Survivor

Through the labyrinth of my dreams, a voice made it into my consciousness, startling me awake. I wasn't sure what they'd said, but when I opened my eyes, there was no one there. My limbs trembled in the cold, dark air. The rope around my wrists made it impossible to warm myself.

Holding my breath, I listened for more voices, but before another came, a key clicked in the lock and the door creaked open.

Like an oasis in the desert, a large form in a black hoodie stepped into the room, the silhouette unmistakable.

"Ba... Bane?" Even in my delirious state, I knew not to use his real name, not where others could hear. I shifted on the chair, yanking on my binds.

"Scarlett." His voice was only a breath, but the moment it met my ears, a sob burst from my lips. The magnitude of emotion was too much for my body to hold back.

Taking one more look around the hallway, he stepped into the room, hurrying to my side. "Shh, it's okay. I'm here now."

"Thank you. Thank you." With blood still dripping from his knife, he sliced through the rope around my hands. I inhaled his scent as he leaned in close to me, tears trailing down my cheeks. "I didn't think—"

"Save your strength." The moment my hands were free, he wrapped his arms around me and pulled to his body. "We need to get out of here."

I nodded, submitting to his kiss when he pressed his lips to mine. The touch was much too brief, but I knew we needed to move.

"Stay close to me."

With my hand in his, we left my prison behind, my heart pounding as we pushed through the dim, dank hallways of the compound. The eerie silence played on my nerves, revving up my paranoia, but Bane moved with lethal grace, his muscles tense and poised for action.

"Stay close," he whispered, his warm breath on my ear sending shivers down my spine. Pressing another kiss to my lips, he placed his knife in my hand before pulling his gun out of its holster. "I love you, Little Red. I will always come for you."

His words sent my heart into a cartwheel, but I had no time to process the emotion before he started moving forward again.

Numerous doors lined either side of us as we walked on silent feet down the concrete halls, but it wasn't until we turned the corner that distant footsteps and murmured conversations echoed through the building.

A door opened ahead, and Bane quickly pulled me behind a stack of crates, pressing my back against the cold wall. We held our breaths, waiting for the intruder to pass. The moment they did, Bane slipped out from behind him, pulling another knife from his pocket and stabbing the guard in the neck.

A shudder wracked through my body as I watched him take the man's life, but I felt no remorse. They were all evil and deserved what they got.

With the dead guard's body sprawled on the ground, Bane reached for my hand and took a few steps toward the exit when I heard the unmistakable voices of Victor, Joshua, and my father engaged in a heated conversation. My heart was like a heavy weight, anchoring me to the floor as I strained my ears to hear what was being said. But as quickly as my body froze, it thawed. Before Bane could stop me, I darted ahead, peeking into the crack where the guard had left the door slightly ajar.

"Ah, Scarlett," Victor sneered, sending ice through my veins as he stepped into view and pushed the door open wider. "So glad you could join us."

Behind him, my father's expression was pure horror when he caught sight of me. A towering figure, who I assumed was his bodyguard, stood beside him.

Victor took a step closer, but Bane wrapped his arm around my body and pulled me aside, positioning himself in front of me with his gun in Victor's face. "Stay away from her."

When Victor took a step back, I caught a glimpse of my husband standing beside him with a gun aimed at my father. I tried to get around Bane, but he wouldn't budge.

"Joshua," I stammered, unable to hide the tremor in my voice. "You won't get away with this."

"Ah, my lovely wife," Joshua replied, his tone mocking. "You'd be surprised what I can get away with."

"Scarlett, stay behind me," Bane whispered only seconds before the room erupted into chaos. Joshua opened fire on my father and his bodyguard, bullets ripping through the air like lethal hailstones. Using the momentary distraction, Victor darted for a stack of crates and Bane returned fire, shielding me with his body.

"Stay down!" Bane yelled at me, his voice barely audible above the cacophony of gunfire and shouts. My heart hammered, fear making it difficult to breathe. I crouched low, trying to make myself as small a target as possible.

"Scarlett, you need to get out of here!" My father's voice rang out from across the room as he hid behind one of the rusted machines, concern etched in his silver-haired features as he fired another round. His bodyguard stood beside him, his square jaw tense as he engaged in the firefight.

Continuing to provide cover, Bane pushed me out of the doorway. "Go! Now!"

For a moment, I just stood there, a cool numbness washing over my body as I debated what to do. I couldn't leave him there—couldn't leave my father—but before I could take a single step, a bullet struck my father's bodyguard in the shoulder, causing him to cry out in pain.

In that moment, everything seemed to slow down, and amidst the chaos, Victor spotted an opening and lunged for my father, seizing him by the arm and pressing a gun to his temple. The room fell silent, the gunfire ceasing as everyone froze, their attention locked on the standoff.

"Drop your weapons, or I'll blow his brains out!" Victor snarled, his eyes wide with madness. Bane hesitated, his blue eyes filled with conflict as he seemed to weigh his options. "Do it, now!"

"Scarlett," Bane murmured under his breath, his expression full of regret. "I'm sorry."

"Please don't let him kill my father," I whispered back, my voice shaking. It felt like the world was collapsing around me, and there was nothing I could do to stop it. He stood protectively in front of me, shielding me from any potential danger, but I could feel his muscles tense at my words.

"Enough!" Victor snarled, his impatience reaching its peak. He tightened his grip on my father's arm, the barrel of the gun digging into his skin. "This is all so... *pathetic.*"

"Let him go, Victor," Bane growled, his voice low and dangerous. Coming out from behind his hiding spot, Joshua pointed his gun at my father as well, the look on his face turning my stomach. My father had done so much for him over the years. Seeing him so willing to take my father's life made me realize how little I really knew him.

"Joshua, you're a coward!" I screamed, my fear giving way to fury. "You've always been a coward, and you'll never change!"

"Shut up, Scarlett!" Joshua snarled back, his eyes wild as he glared at me from across the room.

"Please..." My voice trembled as I pleaded with Joshua. "Don't let him hurt my father."

My eyes turned to my father's old business partner. "Victor, please don't do this," I pleaded, desperate for a resolution that wouldn't end in bloodshed. But as I looked into Victor's eyes, I realized there would be no reasoning with him.

"Last chance," Victor hissed, pressing the gun harder against my father's temple.

"Joshua, please," I whispered, hopelessness seeping into my words. "If there's any humanity left in you, let him go."

"Humanity?" Joshua scoffed. "That was never part of the deal."

"Enough!" Victor barked. In one fluid movement, he released my father, pushing him to the ground. "You have served your purpose, Mr. Prejean. Your time is up."

Before any of us could react, Victor turned his gun on Joshua and pulled the trigger, sending a bullet tearing through Joshua's head. He crumpled to the floor, blood pooling around his lifeless body. The sound of the gunshot echoed through the room, leaving a ringing in my ears and bile burning up my throat.

"Joshua!" I screamed, choking on the name as tears blurred my vision, my body doubling over. My world went dark, swirling in a vortex of my emotions. Bane's strong arms wrapped around me, his warmth the only thing grounding me in the horrifying reality.

"Scarlett," he whispered into my ear. "I promise you, we're going to get out of here. I won't let anyone else hurt you."

My heart twisted in my chest as I stared at Joshua's lifeless body. A storm of emotions raged within me—relief, grief, and an unsettling sense of liberation. For so long, I'd been trapped under his thumb, afraid of what he might do to me if I ever tried to escape. But now... now he was gone, and the chains binding me for years were finally broken. Victor's gun, however, was once again aimed at my father, so we weren't out of the woods yet.

I nodded, still trying to process everything that had just happened, my limbs paralyzed by shock. A cold, triumphant smirk appeared on Victor's face as he stood over my father. It was clear we needed to act quickly, but my legs felt like lead, weighted down by my internal turmoil.

"Victor!" Bane's voice cut through the chaos. "Let her father go!"

"Or what?" Victor sneered, pressing the barrel of his gun against my father's temple. "You'll kill me? I can shoot him before your bullet hits flesh."

The rage in Bane's eyes remained steady even as he replied, "Maybe, but I can still take you with me."

Keeping his gaze locked on Bane, Victor said, "Go ahead, try it."

In that moment of confusion, as everyone focused on Bane and Victor's standoff, something changed. It was almost imperceptible, but I felt a ripple of tension in the air, a sudden shift in power.

Then, without warning, Bane lunged at Victor. Without his support, I fell to my knees, trying to make sense of the scene in front of me. I flinched as the sound of gunfire split the air, praying that Bane hadn't been hit, but when the dust settled, it was Victor who lay motionless on the floor, a bullet hole between his eyes. Standing over him, Bane stared at the man who had held me hostage, his chest heaving.

His focus shifting, Bane darted across the room, reaching his hand out to help me off the ground. "Scarlett, it's time to get out of here."

CHAPTER 40

The Survivor

B ane led the way, his hand gripping mine tightly as we weaved through the maze of corridors, our steps echoing off the walls. My father and his injured bodyguard followed closely behind but took a different exit. The flickering of flashlights cast eerie shadows that seemed to dance around us, as if mocking our desperate escape.

"Stay close to me," Bane whispered, his grip on my hand tightening. His palm was warm against mine, and it provided a small comfort amidst the chaos.

A moment later, we burst out of the compound together, the cold night air stinging my cheeks as we sprinted toward his car. Across the courtyard, I caught a glimpse of my father and his injured bodyguard also making their escape. I flashed a sad smile at him as he and his bodyguard climbed into their vehicle.

Bane held my hand tightly and we ran through the dark alley, our breaths coming in ragged gasps. My heart was pounding so hard I thought it might burst from my chest, but I kept going despite my fading energy.

"Are you okay?" Bane called out over the sound of our footsteps and rain.

I nodded, my throat too tight to speak. The adrenaline was still pumping through my veins, making it difficult to focus on anything else. We had reached the outside unseen, the night sky like an inky cloak above us. The air held the faint tang of the nearby river and smells of the city, and never had freedom felt so sweet. I was okay.

As we rounded a corner, Bane suddenly pulled me into another alleyway and his black sedan came into view, parked behind a dumpster.

"Get in." Bane said, unlocking the car doors. I fumbled with the handle, finally managing to pull it open and slide inside. My heart pounded in my ears, my fight or flight instinct telling me to keep running, but Bane didn't get into the car with me. Instead, he opened the trunk, shutting it after a few moments.

"Bane! What are you doing?" Tremors wracked my body, my teeth chattering more from anxiety than from the cold air. "We need to get out of here!"

A second later, he popped his head into the car, pressing his lips to mine for a kiss that wasn't nearly long enough. "Stay here and lock the doors, Little Red. I'm going to set this bitch on fire. I'll be right back. Then, when the ashes settle, you can come back and blow them away."

Before I had a chance to argue—to tell him to get in the car and drive before we got caught—he took off again.

I locked the car's doors, sliding back in my seat and trying to make myself as invisible as I could. The moments between when he left and when he returned felt like hours, but I knew it had only been minutes—minutes where my head was on a swivel, watching all angles of the car to make sure no one had found us.

I jolted when he returned and knocked on the window, the intrusion catching me by surprise and taking me a heartbeat to unlock the door.

A moment later, the engine roared to life as Bane floored the gas pedal, tires screeching against the pavement as we sped away down the dark alley.

As the distillery went up in flames in the rearview mirror, I glanced over at Bane, his jaw clenched, and eyes focused on the road ahead. His tattoos seemed to come alive in the dim glow of the dashboard lights, a constant reminder of the darkness that surrounded him. Reaching out, he interlaced his fingers with mine, reminding me that everything about him was perfect for me.

"Thank you," I whispered, my voice barely audible above the hum of the engine. "For everything."

352

He glanced at me, his eyes softening for a moment before returning to the road. "We're in this together, Little Red. *Forever.* I'll always be there for you."

My heart fluttered as I leaned across the center console to kiss him on the cheek. "I love you, too, Ethan. I just wanted you to know that. And you are good enough for me."

Glancing at me again, his clear blue eyes shone with his grin. He lifted my hand to his mouth and kissed my knuckles. "And I love you, too, *mon joli petit amant.* very much." My pretty little lover. Cajun French was a dying language, so to hear those words out of him took me completely by surprise. Thanks to my great grandmother, I knew many of the words—mostly the swear ones.

My cheeks heated and I slid back into my seat, glancing back out of my window at the barely visible blaze in the distance. "Where are we going?"

"Somewhere safe outside of the city until things die down," Bane replied, kissing my hand again. "Phantom made a temporary power outage just as we were leaving, so no security cameras in that area would have seen our car, but from the looks of the fiery scene, the police are likely to chalk it up as a Mob shootout. I don't see them suspecting anyone else has been there."

As sirens screamed in the distance, which wasn't uncommon for New Orleans on a good night, we drove for what felt like hours, weaving through the backstreets of the city. I tried to calm my racing thoughts, but the image of Joshua's lifeless body kept creeping back into my mind.

"Scarlett," Bane's voice interrupted my thoughts, his eyebrows furrowing. "Are you okay?"

I shrugged, tears welling up in my eyes as my emotions shifted. "I don't know," I whispered. "It's just... everything that's happened. It's a lot to process."

Bane reached across the console, caressing my cheek. "I know, but we made it out alive, love. That's something, isn't it?"

I nodded, feeling a small glimmer of hope amidst the disarray. Maybe there was a chance for us to start over, to build a new life together. After everything, it was all I wanted, so I clung to that hope like a lifeline. The world outside was a blur of darkness and uncertainty, but in that small, stolen moment in time, I grasped onto the hope that maybe, just maybe, we'd find a way to overcome our demons and forge a new path together.

After some time, Bane turned down a quiet side street and cut the engine. In the sudden silence, he turned to look at me. The moonlight illuminated his face, showcasing the bruises and marks from all the fights he'd gotten into over the past days to save me, but his face still took my breath away.

Leaning forward, he brushed a strand of hair from my eyes. "Are you okay? Really okay?"

I nodded, the tenderness of his touch sending warmth blooming in my chest. "Thanks to you, I'll be okay."

Seeming unable to hold back any longer, he pulled me into his arms until I was straddling him in his seat. I melted against him, finally letting my emotions free as tears spilled down my cheeks.

"I thought I'd never see you again," I whispered, the memory of that pain bringing it back to my chest.

"I'll always find you," he murmured into my hair as his hand ran over my knotty locks. "No matter what."

Drawing back, he gazed into my eyes and I lost myself in their depths. "You're everything to me, Little Red. *Everything.*"

My hand went up to caress his cheek, loving the way his stubble felt below my fingers. "And you're my hero. My love. *Mon amant assassin.*" My assassin lover.

Chuckling, he brought his lips to mine, wrapping his arm around my back and pulling me closer until I was nearly on his lap.

Overcome with emotion, I deepened the kiss, trying to convey all the fear, relief, and passion that had been building inside me. He returned it fervently, our bruised bodies fitting together like two broken pieces made whole.

"The moment I saw you in the bookstore, *mon joli petit amant*" he said, pulling away just enough to look into my eyes, his forehead leaning against mine. "I knew I would move heaven and earth to keep you by my side. You were my light in the darkness. My reason for being. I fought it at first because I wanted to keep you safe from me, but I will never let you go again."

CHAPTER 41

The Survivor

O ur weary feet crunched over the gravel as we approached the safe house, hidden behind dense foliage just outside of New Orleans. Bane's firm, reassuring hand held mine as we stumbled through the dark. Still present was a mixture of relief and lingering fear that left me both alive and vulnerable.

"Almost there," he murmured, his voice rough from shouting orders and fighting for our lives. The moonlight caught the angles of his face, illuminating his eyes.

"Thank you, baby," I whispered, his hand giving mine a reassuring squeeze.

When we reached the front door, Bane... *Ethan*... retrieved a key from his pocket, quickly unlocking it. We stepped inside, the musty scent of disuse immediately hitting my nostrils. Our bodies still hummed with adrenaline, the aftereffects of the blood-pumping battle we'd just fought. My muscles ached and screamed, but I couldn't bring myself to care. All that mattered was that we were alive.

"Are you alright?" he asked, genuine concern lacing his voice as he scanned me for any visible injuries. His gaze lingered on the bruises and cuts marring my skin.

"I'm fine," I lied, not wanting to burden him with my pain. "Just a little shaken."

"Scarlett, don't lie to me." He lifted my chin with his fingers, his eyes never leaving mine. "You've been through hell tonight. It's okay to admit that you're hurting."

I sighed, conceding defeat. "Alright, maybe I'm not completely fine. But I'll heal."

"Let's get you cleaned up." He guided me toward the small bathroom. The flickering overhead light illuminated the cracked tile floor, so much different from our cottage in Alabama, but I was grateful for any semblance of normalcy after the chaotic night we'd experienced.

As I washed off the grime and blood clinging to my skin, I couldn't help but be lost in thought about this man who had saved me. He had shown me a side of himself few people had seen—a gentle, caring protector who would do whatever he could to protect me. I knew, however, beneath that tenderness lay a skilled assassin, a man who had taken lives and navigated the darkest corners of humanity for years. How could one person be so contradictory?

After we were both clean, he wrapped me in a towel, leading me to the only bedroom in the cottage.

Standing in the dimly lit bedroom, I could feel Ethan's eyes on me, studying my body with a mixture of concern and desire. The adrenaline from our battle against the Mob was still coursing through my veins, making me feel more alive than ever, but it had taken its toll.

"Scarlett," he murmured, his fingers gently tracing over a particularly nasty bruise on my ribcage. "You're hurt."

"I'll be okay," I reassured him, wincing at the tenderness of his touch. "What about you?"

He shrugged, attempting to brush off the question, but I wasn't going to let him off that easily. Stepping closer to him, I ran my hand over the hard planes of his chest and felt the scars hidden beneath the inked canvas of his skin. Each one told a story of survival and pain, of the price he'd paid for the life he'd chosen.

"Your body has been through so much," I whispered, my fingertips brushing against a jagged scar above his heart. "Yet here you are, still standing, still fighting."

"Only because of you." His voice was husky and raw. "I wouldn't have made it this far without you, *mon joli petit amant*. I'd do anything to keep you safe."

The words sent shivers down my spine, and I could not take my gaze away from his piercing blue eyes. As if sensing my needs, he guided me to the bed, climbing in next to me. Moonlight filtered through the curtains, casting an ethereal light that soothed my frayed nerves.

"Then let me take care of you," I whispered, pressing a tender kiss to the scar beneath my fingers. "You need it as much as I do."

He watched me intently as I laid out the contents of the first aid kit on the bed, never looking away from my movements as I dipped a cotton ball in antiseptic and held it toward a slice on his hand. "Are you ready?"

"Always," he replied in the deep, velvety tone that soothed, yet ignited me.

Taking a deep breath, I cleaned his wounds, my touch as gentle as I could make it when my hands were still shaking. Although his body grew tense with every wound I dabbed at, he never winced or flinched. Instead, he watched me, a mixture of gratitude and something deeper, more profound, in his gaze.

When I was finished, he took a fresh cotton ball and murmured, "Your turn."

His hands, so rough when they needed to be, were also incredibly tender, as if he was pouring all his love and care into every touch, every swipe of a cotton ball, every bandage.

"Thank you," I whispered, feeling the sting of the antiseptic fade away under his touch. "For everything."

There were a thousand unspoken words that passed between us in that instant as our eyes locked. I knew without a doubt that we had found something extraordinary in each other, as unlikely as that seemed.

"Scarlett, you don't have to thank me. I would do it all again in a heartbeat."

"Promise me." My heart pounded.

"Always," he assured me, sealing his promise with a tender kiss on my lips. "No matter what life throws at us, I'll always be there for you."

With the last bandage secured, the magnetic attraction grew stronger between us. I lay back on the bed and he crawled over me, never breaking eye contact as his eyes filled with a storm of emotions mirroring my own.

"Little Red." His lips brushed against mine, sending shivers down my spine. "I need you."

"Show me."

Threading my fingers into his hair, I pulled him closer, our kisses hungry–*desperate*. His strong hands gripped my hips, pulling me even closer as if determined to erase any distance between us. The taste of him was intoxicating, and I couldn't get enough.

'Tell me what you want," he whispered, his voice a tempting growl that sent heat rising in my body.

The fire burning within me was fueled by the intensity of our connection, and only he could quench it. "Touch me." My voice was a mere breath as I rolled my body against him.

Taking his time, he glided his fingers over my skin like a master painter working on a masterpiece. Each brush of his fingertips ignited my body as though it were a flaming match. I reciprocated, feeling both his strength and vulnerability as my hands traced along his muscular form. It was when I traced the tattoos adorning his body that I was struck by how much they reflected his life—a life shaped by darkness, pain, and sacrifice.

"Your touch is like magic," he confessed, his breath hot against my ear as he continued to explore my body with reverence. "I've never felt anything like this."

"Neither have I." Although we hadn't known each other for long, my heart swelled with love for the man who'd helped me discover my own strength. "We're in this together, Ethan."

"Always," he whispered, his eyes locked on mine. Ethan's lips trailed down my neck, sending electricity through to my core.

"I need you, Little Red," he murmured between kisses.

"Then, take me."

A groan of approval accompanied his lips as they moved from my neck, pulling the towel off me with his hand. As I writhed beneath him, he teased my nipples, taking each one into his mouth and lavishing attention on them. He continued to descend, trailing kisses down my chest and stomach before settling between my thighs.

For a tantalizing moment, he stared at my center, his hot breath fanning across my sensitive skin. "You're so beautiful, *mon joli petit amant*. Perfect."

Then he was on me. His touch was electric, the swirl of his tongue around my clit sending waves of pleasure through me. His movements were slow and deliberate, as if he were savoring every moment as much as I was. My body trembled, my head falling back as my hips rolled of their own accord. He sucked and licked at my clit as his fingers penetrated inside me, forcing a moan to tear from my lips.

"Ethan... *please.*"

My core pulsed around his fingers, my orgasm teasing me right to the edge. His fingers rubbed that sensitive spot inside of me as I fought against his grasp on my hips.is lips sealed around my clit, and I doubled down his efforts as I ground my pussy against his face. When I finally tipped over the edge, I cried out, the iron heat sweeping over me, causing my whole body to tremble with euphoria.

When my tremors eased, he crawled back over my body, pressing his lips against mine.

"Gods, you're amazing," he breathed, his eyes darkening. "You're so beautiful like this."

Every other thought left my mind when he leaned down again to kiss me, his presence taking over every one of my senses.

Slipping his hand between us, he guided his hard length inside me. The way his girth stretched me was a delicious pressure, making both of us groan at how exquisite it felt.

With deep thrusts, he worked himself deeper until there was no space not filled with him—no space left in me to feel any pain or remorse. It was only him. And as he rolled his hips slowly and thoroughly, sending waves of pleasure coursing through me until my cheeks tingled, I knew he was all I would ever want.

Moving his hands to my hips, Ethan's grip tightened as he took me harder, the headboard slamming against the wall with every collision of our bodies. I lifted my hips to meet his as I chased another orgasm, the coil in my belly tightening until I could no longer hold back.

With Ethan's name on my lips, I screamed as my orgasm washed over me in an intense wave, my body quivering. I clung to him as my body pulsed around him, the clench of my pussy bringing him to his own climax.

With a guttural groan, he released himself into me, warming my insides with his seed. When the tension in his body eased, his kisses languid, our bodies trembling as we both came down from the clouds.

CHAPTER 42

The Survivor

TWO WEEKS LATER

The scent of fresh beignets and coffee greeted me as I walked out of the bedroom in Ethan's apartment—the apartment that became mine as well the moment we'd left the safehouse. After he and I had narrowly escaped with our lives, we'd remained in the cabin outside New Orleans for four days, healing from our wounds, both physical and psychological, while connecting on a level I'd never shared with Joshua. A huge part of my own healing was staying away from the media, but Phantom kept an eye on the news coverage for the two fires and bodies found in the ashes. Although the investigation was ongoing, all reports chalked it up to a rival gang war. From what he gathered from the coverage and reports he hacked into, the authorities were not looking into anyone outside of that.

When I made my way into the kitchen, his black t-shirt loosely hanging off my shoulder, Ethan was already awake, standing at the kitchen counter arranging a tray of pastries.

His tattooed arms flexed as he turned, flashing me a smile that made my heart skip.

"Morning, Little Red," he said, his hair still tousled from sleep. "Thought we'd start the day off right."

Crossing the room, I leaned up on my toes to kiss him, savoring the sweet taste of powdered sugar on his lips. "You're going to spoil me."

"That's the plan."

With our cups of coffee and a plate of what amounted to pure sugar, we settled on the balcony overlooking the street below. The wrought iron felt cool under my palms as I soaked in the city, its energy thrumming through my veins. After all I'd been through at my own house, I never wanted to live there again, but Ethan's apartment was close to work, so it had been a no-brainer. After everything we'd endured, it felt surreal to finally be there together, starting a new chapter in our lives. No more looking over our shoulders. No more violence and fear. Just him and me, wrapped in the blanket of our new life.

Almost too soon, he squeezed my hand, flashing me one of those devilish smiles that made my knees weak. "Time to go, love. Don't want to be late."

My stomach fluttered with nerves and excitement as I brushed my teeth and pulled on my clothes. He was taking me to meet his family—the niece he adored enough to risk his life for, and the sister that meant the world to him. Although he'd assured me repeatedly I didn't have to be nervous, I wanted to make a good impression and show them that I was worthy of him. It was funny how the tables had turned. For weeks, it had always been him who insisted he wasn't good enough for me, but I never shared that opinion. Feeling for him the way I did now, I was so grateful I hadn't listened to him.

Walking into the bathroom, already dressed in his signature black hoodie and jeans, he seemed to read my thoughts. "They're going to love you like I do, *mon joli petit amant*. Just be yourself."

I nodded, breathing deep to calm my nerves as we headed out the door.

The hospital loomed large and imposing as we walked through the sliding doors. The scent of antiseptic stung my nose as the hush of quiet voices blanketed the lobby. I'd been to the same hospital several times before, so I knew it was the best, but going into it to see a very sick child twisted my insides. So many of us live our lives never thinking about the children in the Pediatric Intensive Care Units or children's hospitals—we never have to bear witness to sick children—*truly* sick children—and I knew it would break my heart to see it.

Ethan gave my hand a reassuring squeeze as he guided me toward the elevator. "This way."

My heels clicked against the speckled tiles, each step ratcheting up my anxiety. What if his family didn't approve? What if I couldn't connect with his niece? Doubt swirled like a gathering storm. Bane had quickly become my everything, and I his, and I wanted his family to accept me as their own.

The elevator doors slid open, and we stepped inside the cramped space. As we ascended, Bane brushed his fingers against my cheek, whispering in my ear, "It's going to be okay."

I nodded, willing myself to believe him. I wasn't just worried about myself, but about his niece also.

The doors opened again, revealing a long hallway lined with rooms. Monitors beeped and nurses bustled by, their rubber soles squeaking.

Leading me to a door halfway down, Ethan turned around to face me, planting a small kiss on my lips. "Ready?"

I inhaled slowly, steadying my nerves before nodding. "Ready."

With no more hesitation, he pushed open the door and we stepped inside.

Morning light filtered through half-drawn blinds, falling in slanted bars across the bed. Beneath a maze of wires and tubes lay a small, fragile girl with the top of her bald head wrapped in gauze. Her skin held a grayish pallor, but her eyes shone bright as they fixed on her uncle. Just seeing her in that state, but still smiling, brought a smile to my own face, warmth blooming in my chest.

"Uncle Ethan!" she cried, her voice hoarse but delighted.

Letting go of my hand, he rushed forward, enveloping the little girl in a gentle hug. "Hey, troublemaker. Told you I'd come back, and what did I promise to bring you?"

With a brilliant grin on her face, she pulled away from him, looking around his back to where he was holding a stuffed pink llama in his hand.

"My llama!" she squealed as she held out her hands.

Bringing my hand to my mouth, I stifled a giggle at their interaction even as it made my ovaries explode. Ethan would be an amazing daddy, and I fully intended to let him impregnate me.

Over his shoulder, the little girl's gaze met mine, and despite her sickness, a glimmer of light shone there.

Reflecting her smile, I approached the bed. "Hi, Evelyn. I'm Scarlett. It's so nice to meet you."

Her eyes widened slightly. "You're Uncle Ethan's friend?"

I nodded, touched by the sweet lilt of her voice. "That's right. He's told me so many wonderful things about you. I hear you're incredibly brave."

Pink spots appeared on her pale cheeks as she gave a small shrug. "The medicine makes me sleepy, and sometimes I get scared." Her voice dropped to a whisper as she squeezed the llama to her chest. "But I don't tell anybody that."

My heart melted. Perching carefully on the edge of the bed beside Ethan, I took her small hand in mine. "It's okay to feel scared sometimes. Even brave girls like you, but you know what?" I leaned into her, whispering conspiratorially, "A little secret? I get scared too. All the time."

"You do?" Her mouth spread into a toothy smile, the two in the front missing in action.

"Oh, yes. More than I'd like to admit." I smiled ruefully. "But you know what helps me when I'm afraid?"

She shook her head, leaning in closer.

"Having people who care about me. Like your Uncle Ethan." I nodded toward him. "And now you too. Because if we stick together, we don't have to be afraid. Not really."

Evelyn considered this for a moment, then gave my hand a determined squeeze. "And my mommy too!"

For the next several minutes, I remained on the bed next to Evie as she told me all about her new llama, giving it a name and letting me hold it. Bane watched us from across the room, a mix of emotions playing across his rugged features. Relief. Pride. And something deeper that made my heart skip.

As Evelyn's eyes started to droop with fatigue, I helped her lay down, covering her with her blanket. Once her eyes were closed, I stood and crossed over to him. He wrapped an arm around my waist, his touch anchoring me.

"How's she doing today?" I asked, my voice just above a whisper. "Did the nurse give you an update?"

Bane sighed, the corners of his mouth turning down. "The same. Her blood counts are still low. But..." His eyes flicked back to Evelyn. "She seems happier since you got here. And she's conscious, so that's a good sign."

Leaning into him, I took comfort in his solid strength. "She's an amazing kid. So resilient. And beautiful too. She certainly loves her Uncle Ethan."

Nodding, his jaw tightened. "Yeah. Yeah, she is, and that, she does. She's very special to me. My sister and Evie were the only family I had left... until you came into my life."

His words brought so much warmth to my chest, but I only responded with a smile and a kiss, letting him pull me into his side.

We stood in silence for a moment, the steady beep of monitors and hushed voices of the ICU enveloping us. Although her mother wasn't in the room, I imagined Caroline would return soon.

"Bane?"

His eyes met mine, sea glass blue and deep as the ocean.

"I'm here for you. Both of you." I squeezed his hand, willing him to understand what I couldn't yet say out loud. That I would stay by his side through all his darkness, accept his darkness, just as he'd stayed with me through mine.

The lines on his forehead smoothed ever so slightly, and he lifted my hand to his lips.

"I know, and I'll do the same for you. We're in this together, Little Red. You're now part of my family too. All you need now, or when you're ready, is my ring on your finger."

Just as my heart flipped at what had almost seemed like a proposal, his sister's voice broke the moment.

"She's right, you know."

We both turned to see Caroline standing in the doorway, a tired smile on her face. Crossing over to us, she placed a hand on Bane's shoulder.

"I don't think I've ever seen Evelyn this happy before," she continued, blinking back tears. "The way her face lit up when you and Scarlett walked in..."Caroline took my hand in both of hers, squeezing gently. "Thank you for being here. For bringing that light back into her eyes." She glanced between Ethan and me. "For both of them."

The words made my heart swell, and I had to swallow the lump in my throat before I could speak. "Of course. Ethan has lit up my life just as much as I've lit up his, and I'm just so glad I could meet the both of you. She's a fighter, that one."

Caroline nodded, pride and pain mingling in her expression. "That she is."

We stood in a circle then, hands clasped together, drawing strength from one another. Evelyn lay sleeping, her chest rising and falling steadily, the monitor beeping in a rhythmic lullaby.

At that moment, we were no longer alone on our individual journeys. We had become a family, bound by hope and love. And together, we would make it through the darkness into the light.

CHAPTER 43

The Survivor

ONE MONTH LATER

The brass bell above the door chimed as I stepped into my Tangled in the Pages, its familiar melody sending a wave of nostalgia washing over me. Excitement and nervousness fluttered in my chest like dueling butterflies, unsure whether to take flight or remain grounded. My eyes scanned the cozy interior, drinking in the sight of the shelves brimming with stories waiting to be discovered. With the media and investigation surrounding Joshua's death, I hadn't stepped into my bookstore in a month, but with Christmas right around the corner, my store needed me. If I were to be honest, I needed it as well.

"Scarlett!" In the stillness of the not-yet-open bookstore, Ashley's voice pierced through the silence. She rushed over to me, her black curls bouncing with every step. "You're back!"

The sight of her made me feel like I was choked by the emotions welling up inside of me. Having been away from these walls for so long, it was like returning home to the solace of the books, and the warmth of the employees that have turned into my family. "Hey, Ash."

A moment later, Jack appeared from behind a bookshelf, his eyes brightening as he noticed me. It didn't take long for his tall, lanky frame to close the distance. It was like receiving a balm for my bruised heart when they both wrapped their arms around me.

"Welcome back, Scarlett," Jack said, his stoic exterior cracking beneath the relief in his voice.

"I missed you guys," I choked out, tears streaming down my cheeks. Having their unwavering support meant the world to me, and I couldn't help but think how lucky I was to have them.

"Alright, enough with the waterworks," Ashley said in her no-nonsense manager voice, breaking our embrace and wiping away her own tears. "Let's settle you in and catch up on all the gossip you missed. One of our new seasonal employees is a hot mess."

I laughed, shaking my head. "I'm sure Manager Ashley can whip her into shape."

With the side-eye she shot at me, I realized I needed to know more about this new employee. Anything to get my mind off the drama of my own life. I was just relieved that things had finally started to settle down.

"Scarlett," Jack said, drawing me back to the present, "just remember that we're here for you. If you need anything or if you want to talk about... well, anything, just let us know."

I nodded, patting him on the back. "Thank you, Jack."

With opening time fast approaching, I pulled on my apron and took my place behind the counter, ready to dive back into the world of books and coffee—ready to see my regulars again and create a new routine no longer shadowed by an abusive husband.

Watching Ashley and Jack flit about the store, completing their opening procedures like a well-oiled machine, I couldn't help but smile. "I can't thank you both enough for everything you've done while I was away," I said, my eyes welling up with tears as I took in their warm smiles. "Your support means the world to me."

"Hey, that's what friends are for," Ashley chimed in, beaming at me from across the room, opening the door and allowing the trickle of customers in.

For the next few hours, I busied myself behind the counter, catching up with my regulars and refamiliarizing myself with working in my own store. Since the night Bane had taken me from my home in the night, I had been gone for more than two months, so there was a lot I had to catch up on. I was grateful to Ashley and Jack for taking care of my store as though it was their own and running it in my absence without incident.

"The usual?" I asked as the next customer approached, a man who'd been coming into my store since the day I'd opened it.

Henry's eyes crinkled behind his wire-rimmed glasses and he nodded. "Yes, but this time you'll take my money, Miss Scarlett. I'm happy to see you've returned."

Turning around, I filled a coffee cup with dark roast, setting it in front of him and taking the crisp five-dollar bill in his hand. "I'll take your money, but I'll put it in the tip drawer for my employees."

With another smile, he pulled another bill out of his bill fold. "In that case, I'll sweeten the pot. They've certainly taken care of me in your absence."

He walked to his favorite spot by the window. I savored the warmth that spread through me at the sight of my customers all enjoying what I'd built. It meant so much to me to be a part of their lives.

The late afternoon sun filtered through the bookstore windows, casting a warm golden glow over the shelves and customers browsing their contents. My heart swelled with contentment as I watched Ashley help a young couple pick out a Christmas gift for their parents. The simple act of assisting someone in finding the perfect book brought me so much joy. I glanced at Jack, who was expertly arranging a display of holiday-themed novels near the entrance, his dedication evident in his focused expression. At that moment, I couldn't help but feel an overwhelming sense of gratitude for my incredible friends.

"Scarlett," Ashley whispered as she approached me, her eyes twinkling mischievously. "I think you have a visitor."

Curiosity piqued, I followed her gaze to the front door where Ethan stood, leaning against the frame with his arms crossed and a playful smile on his lips. He twirled a single red rose in one of his hands, which meant so much more than my friends realized. Joshua had always given me flowers after abusing me—an apology for something I would never forgive, and he would do again. Ethan, on the other hand, had nothing to apologize to me for. He was the most amazing partner I could have ever dreamed up.

My pulse quickened at the sight of him in all his semi-goth sexiness, both excited and nervous about what this unexpected visit could mean. We'd been inseparable since he'd rescued me, but I hadn't expected him to visit me at the store on my first day back.

"Hey there, stranger," I greeted him, trying to sound casual as I approached. "What brings you here?"

"Can't I just come see my favorite bookstore owner, *mon joli petit amant?*" Ethan teased, pushing away from the door and closing the distance between us. His new nickname for me sent a hot flush across my cheeks. "Actually, I have a surprise for you. I packed you a bag. We're leaving for the weekend."

My eyebrows shot up in surprise, and I exchanged a quick glance with Ashley, who was grinning from ear to ear, telling me she must have known about the plan ahead of time. "A weekend getaway?" I asked, the anticipation building in my chest.

"Yep." Nodding, he stepped forward and wrapped his arm around me, pulling me in for a kiss. I could see the amusement on Ashley's face from over his shoulder, but I just smiled and kissed him again. "But I'm not telling you where we're going. You'll have to wait and find out."

His cryptic response only served to fuel my excitement further. Since our relationship began, we'd been through so much together, and the thought of spending a weekend discovering a new place with him was exciting.

"Alright, I'll trust you," I said, meeting his piercing blue eyes. "Give me a few minutes to close up shop, and then we can head out."

"Take your time."

Giving my hand a squeeze, he walked toward the same case of books we'd met in front of, pulling *Treasure Island* off the shelf. With a sexy smile on his face, he brought the book to the sofa in front of the fireplace and sat down to read. I watched him for a moment, realizing it would be difficult for me to get any work done with my sexy man sitting in the same room.

As I turned to inform Ashley and Jack of my sudden departure, their beaming smiles told me they'd both already knew about it. "Did Ethan call the store and let yawl know where he's taking me?"

Instead of answering, Ashley slid her fingers across her lips as though she was zipping her mouth shut.

Jack laughed. "Make sure you text us when you get there." He handed me two cups of freshly brewed coffee; his eyes filled with curiosity. "And take lots of pictures!"

"Of course!" I replied with a grin, taking a sip of the steaming liquid. "I'm sure it's going to be amazing, whatever he has planned. He's thoughtful like that."

Wrapping her arms around me, Ashley pulled me into a hug. "Scarlett, we're so happy for you. You deserve this happiness. Oh..." She paused, turning a glance to where Ethan was sitting. "And he's hot... so definitely take pictures."

I huffed a laugh and planted a kiss on her cheek. "I'll see if I can get one with his shirt off, because you're right. He is hot."

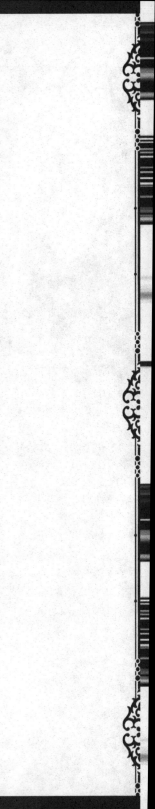

CHAPTER 44

The Survivor

O nce we left my store, we drove for several hours, but it seemed like no time at all. It also didn't take me long to realize we were heading to the Smoky Mountains. I was just glad I hadn't stayed at work until closing time, not that he would have let me, so I wouldn't be exhausted when we got there. The hours passed with playful banter and stories of our pasts, punctuated by me singing badly along to the radio. When the sky began to turn pink and gold, the sun dipping working its way toward the horizon, Ethan turned onto a gravel road that wound up toward the top of the mountain.

"Almost there," he said, squeezing my hand. My heart flipped and flopped in my chest. Although I was looking forward to being back at work, I was even more excited to be going on a new adventure with him—one where the only man with a gun was him.

As we made our way up the road lined on both sides with dense forests, I gazed out the window and took in the beauty around us. We pulled to a stop in front of a secluded cabin hidden among the trees. Streams of golden light poured out through the windows, illuminating the grounds and the log exterior. It didn't look like the kind of place you went to because you *had* to hide out. It looked like the kind of place you went to because you wanted to hide out.

"Wow," I whispered, unable to tear my eyes away from the picturesque scene before me. "This is incredible, Ethan."

Turning off the ignition, he twisted in his seat, leaning forward to kiss me, lingering just long enough to fill my core with heat. "Only the best for you. With all the chaos of the city, I thought you could benefit from some time away. I thought we both could."

With our bags in hand, we crossed the threshold of the cozy cabin, the warmth of the crackling fireplace wrapping around me like a comforting embrace. My gaze wandered to the sliding glass door leading out to a deck where a hot tub bubbled. I loved the cottage we'd stayed at in Alabama, but this one was on a whole other level. I'd never been anywhere like it.

"Has someone been here setting up for us or something?"

Dropping our bags on the floor near the bed, he pulled me into his arms. ""I have my ways of getting things done, Little Red. Are you okay with staying here for a few days?" he asked, his breath warm against my skin. "Or longer?"

I grinned against his chest, the warmth of his body and his scent nearly sending my eyes back into my head. "Thank you. This means more to me than you'll ever know."

When I leaned back to look him in the eyes, he wrapped his arms around my waist and lifted me until my legs were around his waist, pulling me in to kiss him.

The feeling was electric, a jolt that seemed to pass through both of us. His lips were passionate yet tender, and the way he held me close was almost protective. Our hearts beat in unison as his fingers tangled in my hair, sending a delightful shiver down my spine.

Kissing his way from my lips to my ear, he whispered, "It's my duty in life to fill yours with moments that take your breath away and replace every bad memory in your stunning mind with amazing ones."

I thought I might faint from the intensity of emotion that passed between us with his words. He was a lethal man with a poet's soul, my man was the paradox who had my whole heart.

Setting me back on the ground, he reached out to take hold of my hand again and brought it up to his lips to kiss it tenderly. "You're mine now, *mon joli petit amant*. You're mine to protect, to please, to carry you when you're too tired to walk. You're mine, and I am yours."

With my heart full, and his hand in mine, we walked outside to the deck. There was a crackling fire pit nearby, casting flickering shadows over the trees, making me wonder if he'd had someone start the fire before we arrived at the cabin. Knowing Ethan, the refrigerator was also stocked. He always found a way of taking care of everything, even if he wasn't there.

As the crisp mountain air nipped at my cheeks, I inhaled deeply, savoring the scent of pine and smoke that filled the night. It was a reminder of our time in Alabama—the good times.

Approaching the fire, he lowered me into one of the chairs and sat beside me. "I have a surprise for you," he said, a hint of mischief in the twist of his lips.

"Another surprise?" Butterflies swirled in my stomach as I watched him, wondering what he would do next. The weekend getaway had already exceeded my expectations, but I'd learned that he always had something up his sleeves.

"Of course." His blue eyes reflected the fire light. A moment later, he pulled out a small bag containing Graham crackers, marshmallows, and chocolate bars. "A campfire wouldn't be complete without s'mores."

I nodded, stifling a giggle as giddiness flooded me. "I agree."

While the fire blazed in front of us, keeping the December chill, which was so much colder up in the mountains, out of my bones, his arm wrapped around my waist as he told me stories about camping when he was a child. I loved listening to him recount tales of how much trouble he and his sister always got into. Though I felt like I'd known him forever, there was still so much we had to share. I'd met his sister a few times, but I looked forward to the day when Evelyn would be able to leave the hospital and we would be able to do more things as a family.

"Scarlett," he said, drawing my attention away from the fire. It was rare that he called me by my real name, so when he did, I knew whatever he had to say was serious. "There's something I need to tell you."

My heart skipped a beat as I met his gaze, the wire holding my marshmallow lowering to my lap. "What is it?"

The vulnerability in his eyes as he looked into mine took me by surprise. He was always so confident—so strong. I was the vulnerable one.

"You mean so much to me, Little Red," he said, his voice thick with emotion. "Being with you has changed me in ways I never thought possible. I never thought I'd find someone who could understand me, who could see beyond the darkness that surrounds me. But you do. You've shown me that there's more to my life than the shadows that once consumed me. You've shown me what it means to love and be loved, and I can't imagine my life without you."

Before I could respond, my heart hanging on his every word, Ethan took a deep breath, reached into his pocket, and pulled out a small velvet box. My mouth fell open, my heart rate speeding to an erratic pace as he lowered himself on one knee before me, the firelight dancing across his face.

"Scarlett," he said, his voice steady despite the tears brimming in his eyes. "I may still believe you are too good for me, but I will work the rest of my life to be a man who is worthy of you, if you will do me the honor of spending the rest of your life with me?"

I stared at him as the enormity of the moment settled over me. Love, fear, and hope swirled together inside me, leaving me without breath—*without words*. But as I looked at Ethan—this beautiful, broken man who had fought for me, protected me, and loved me—I knew there was only one answer I could give.

"Yes," I whispered, my voice choking on my surge of emotions. "Yes, Ethan. I will marry you."

The End... (unless you read the Extended Epilogue on Book Funnel!)

Enjoy
Saving Scarlett?

If you enjoyed this book, don't forget to
leave a review!

Reviews are vital to authors! They help
books reach new readers. I really
appreciate it!

Leave a review here:
https://www.amazon.com/dp/B0CJR92
XW2

https://www.goodreads.com/book/show
/199751625-saving-scarlett

and go to the link below to read the
Extended Epilogue!
https://dl.bookfunnel.com/ca8ytqgkzz

Also By

Hazel Watson Mystery Series
Kindred Spirits: Prequel
The Sapphire Necklace
Justice for the Slain
Whispers from the Swamp
Crossroads of Death
The Spirit Collector

Crown of the Phoenix Series
Crown of the Phoenix
Crown of the Exiled
Crown of the Prophecy (Coming Soon)
Mate of the Phoenix

Supernatural Savior Series
Song of Death
Goddess of Death

An Other World Series
The Other World
The Other Key
The Other Fate (coming January 2024)

My Alien Mate Series
My Alien Protector

Saving Scarlett

Second Chance with Santa

Acknowledgement

I want to thank my readers for reading my spicy books, and my family for NOT reading my spicy books. I really hope I didn't let you guys down!

I would like to thank my editors, Willow Oak author Services and Kristen N. Winiarski. I know I can be a pain in the ass.

I would like to thank Emily McIntire and H.D. Carlton for giving me the love of dark romance. The first true dark romance I ever read was Haunting Adeline and I fell completely in love. Obviously, after reading all H.D. Carlton's books, I went straight into Emily McIntire's Neverland series, starting with Hooked. Highly Recommend both of these amazing authors!

I also want to thank Stacey Marie Brown for really getting me into the bad boys with weapons and tattoos. Warwick will always be my favorite book boyfriend.

Thank you to Artscandare Book Design and Leigh Graphic Design for working with my scattered mind to get the covers, and special edition covers, all together and beautiful.

About the Author

Raised in a small town in the heart of Louisiana's Cajun Country, C. A. Varian spent most of her childhood fishing, crabbing, and getting sunburnt at the beach. Her love of reading began very young, and she would often compete at school to read enough books to earn prizes.

Graduating with the first of her college degrees as a mother of two in her late twenties, she became a public-school teacher. As of the release of this book, she was finally able to resign from teaching to write full time!

Writing became a passion project, and she put out her first novel in 2021, and has continued to publish new novels every few months since then, not slowing down for even a minute.

Married to a retired military officer, she spent many years moving around for his career, but they now live in central Alabama, with her youngest daughter, Arianna. Her oldest daughter, Brianna, is enjoying her happily ever after with her new husband and several pups. C. A. Varian has two Shih Tzus that she considers her children. Boy, Charlie, and girl, Luna, are their mommy's shadows. She also has three cats named Ramses, Simba, and Cookie.